SECRETS OF VISTAPUR

BENEATH MOONLIT SHADOWS

Rhama Lalgudi Visweswaran

INDIA • SINGAPORE • MALAYSIA

ISBN
Paperback 979-8-89673-771-1
Hardcase 979-8-89724-753-0

Chapter 1

Smitha, Chandra, and Ayisha were finally on their much-awaited vacation to Viridona—a tropical paradise tucked away in the Andaman Sea. It had taken months of juggling calendars, endless group chats, and "What about this weekend?" debates to settle on October. But they had made it. A whole month to themselves, balancing remote work during the weekdays and full-on exploring during the weekends.

Their home base? A cosy two-bedroom Airbnb right in the heart of Vistapur, a seaside town that felt like it belonged in a postcard. The place had everything they'd hoped for: the sound of waves in the distance, local shops that smelled of fresh pastries, and a vibe that whispered, slow down, you're on island time now.

Though, the real gem, was Tavora Forest that was just outside the town. It stretched out like something from an adventure movie—dense, untamed, and completely untouched by human interference. The locals spoke about it with equal parts awe and caution. "It's not just a forest; it's a world of its own," one shopkeeper had told them when they asked for hiking tips.

Despite being so remote, Viridona wasn't exactly off the radar. Vistapur's charm kept the small airport buzzing with adventurers and researchers from all over. But for the three friends, it didn't matter how many people came and went. This was *their* trip, *their* escape from the grind, and they planned to make the most of every moment.

***

"Smitha! Wake up!"

Smitha felt her entire body rock as someone shook her shoulder with growing insistence. The voice was distant at first, muffled by the layers of sleep that clung to her. It grew louder, tugging her out of the cosy fog she was buried in. She groaned, pulling the blanket tighter around herself.

"*Wake up,*" the voice persisted, louder this time.

Smitha cracked her eyes open with monumental effort. It was still heavy with exhaustion. The room was flooded with morning light, far too bright for her current state. She blinked at the blurry but familiar face leaning over her. As the pull of sleep tried to reclaim her, she tugged the blanket over her head, cocooning herself.

Rrrring! Rrrring!

"Wake up!"

The chaos outside her blanket felt distant, but Smitha wished her world could remain like this: a quiet, cosy bubble beneath the covers.

"Where's your phone? Turn off that alarm! It feels like someone's drilling into my skull!" yelled Chandra. Her exasperated voice pierced through the fog of sleep.

Smitha groaned, fumbling beneath her pillow until her fingers brushed against her phone. She squinted at the screen—Alarm: Snooze, Stop. Before she could react, Chandra snatched the phone from her limp hand and angrily tapped the "Stop" button.

"You're impossible," Chandra muttered, rolling her eyes. "How do you even sleep through that? I swear, you are always out the second your head hits the pillow."

"Night safari, remember?" Smitha mumbled, peeking out from under her blanket, her body still aching from the long trek beneath the stars from the night before. "I didn't get to bed until 3 a.m."

"..."

Before Chandra could respond, Smitha added, "Everything felt... surreal. I just collapsed after that long journey."

"Oh, poor you," Chandra said sarcastically. "And now it's almost noon!" she fired back with a grin. "Get up! You're on vacation, not hibernating."

"Get dressed; we're heading for brunch," Ayisha chimed in from the other side of the room. She was already seated on the sofa with her legs crossed. She had tossed aside her magazine and was ready to go. She looked fresh and lively in her pink top and dangling earrings, like a morning flower poised for adventure—quite the opposite of Smitha.

"Good morning to you too!" Smitha called out with a sleepy smile.

With a sigh, she sat up slowly and rubbed her temples. She was finally awake enough to piece together her surroundings. This wasn't their first day in Vistapur—far from it. They had been on the island for over a week now, exploring every hidden corner they could find. Yesterday's night safari had been the crown jewel so far. It was an exhilarating trek through Tavora Forest under the cover of darkness. Magical, yes, but it had left her utterly drained.

She yawned, still trying to shake the heaviness from her limbs. "Just give me five minutes."

"No. No more 'five minutes,'" Ayisha said with a playful smirk. "The food isn't going to wait for you, and neither are we. Come on, sleepyhead!"

Smitha swung her legs over the side of the bed with a resigned sigh. "Fine, fine, I'm getting up. But next time, remind me not to agree to a late-night safari alone. I'm dragging all of you with me."

Chandra raised an eyebrow. "Oh, please. Like I would ever stay up that late to see some animals."

Ayisha chuckled. "I'd love to see you try though. Now, get up—brunch waits for no one!"

***

Fifteen minutes later, the three friends were seated in a cosy restaurant with outdoor seating. The laid-back cushions provided a comfortable setting, while the fresh aroma of coffee mingled with the salty sea breeze. Together, they created the perfect atmosphere for a vacation brunch.

Ayisha leaned back in her chair, basking under the warm sun that filtered through the leaves of the tree above them. "This is life," she exclaimed with a content smile spreading across her face.

Soon, their orders began to arrive. Their lively chatter blended with the clatter of cutlery, enhancing the bustle of the restaurant.

"So, what do we do next?" Chandra asked.

"We've been here for a week and haven't done any shopping. How about we go to the bazaar?" Ayisha suggested enthusiastically.

"I've never seen you buy anything on your shopping sprees. You'll just drag us through every shop," Smitha teased, her tone was light and playful.

"It doesn't matter. I've heard the bazaar has a special Friday market every week. We can treat it like sightseeing, even if we don't buy anything," Ayisha replied, undeterred.

"Well, let's give it a go. It sounds like an immersive experience," Chandra agreed, nodding. "And later in the evening, we can head to that funhouse you've been talking about. Didn't you say it's inside a park?" she added, looking at Smitha.

"Oh yes, the park is supposed to be beautiful. From what I've heard, the sunset is the highlight," Smitha replied.

"Alright, we'll go to the bazaar now, then leave around 4 p.m. and be at the park by 5 p.m. That should give us plenty of time for everything," Ayisha suggested.

"That sounds like a plan. But can I skip the shopping? I'm really tired and could use a nap," Smitha replied, a touch of weariness in her voice.

Ayisha and Chandra exchanged glances before turning to Smitha. "We expected you to say that," Chandra remarked, shaking her head disapprovingly.

"Oh, come on! You guys didn't want to do the night safari, and *I* didn't guilt you into it. To each their own!" Smitha retorted playfully.

"Alright. We'll go to the bazaar and then meet you directly at the funhouse by 5 p.m. Don't sleep in and miss it," Ayisha teased, her voice mock-serious.

"Of course! I'll keep track of the time," Smitha replied, her smile brightening.

Chandra sighed dramatically. "You're hopeless," she said before returning to her meal.

After finishing their meal, they parted ways—Chandra and Ayisha headed to the bazaar while Smitha returned to the apartment.

***

Rrrring! Rrrring!

A few hours later, Smitha heard the alarm blaring once again. She reached out, trying to silence it without leaving her bed. Her efforts were in vain since it was nowhere nearby. Then it struck her: she had placed it on the table across the room, deliberately out of reach, to force herself to get up. With a reluctant sigh, she swung her legs over the side of the bed and trudged across the room to switch it off.

She took a quick shower and got ready in no time. As she prepared to leave, she grabbed her small travel backpack and house keys before stepping out the door. Just as she was about to lock it, she glanced at the clock and noticed the time. It read 4 p.m. A smile crept across her face. *'I'm well ahead of schedule,'* she thought to herself.

***

A few minutes later, Smitha stood at the bus stop, tapping her foot impatiently. Surprisingly, the island was more accessible by public transportation than by any other means. The bus stop to the park was a quick walk from the house. The park wasn't exactly in the heart of Vistapur; rather, it was nestled on the outskirts and bordering the lush Tavora Forest. To get there, she needed to catch a bus that would take her along a scenic coastal road, with the ocean glistening on one side and the forest looming on the other. Eventually, the road would lead to a park renowned for its stunning views of the island's vast greenery.

While she waited, drawn by the aroma of spices wafting through the air, she decided to indulge in a cup of tea from a nearby tea shop. As she sipped the warm brew, she felt the anticipation build—soon, she would be surrounded by nature's beauty, far from the bustling town.

Her bus arrived just as she finished her cup of tea. Smitha boarded and found a seat with a perfect view of the ocean, finally allowing herself to relax. The bus's final stop was the funhouse, giving her a chance to enjoy the ride without worry. She put on her headphones and sank into her seat, letting the music wash over her as she gazed at the breathtaking scenery. The waves sparkled in the sunlight, their rhythmic dance perfectly syncing with the melody of her favourite songs.

Soon, she got off at the bus stop and decided to call Ayisha to check where they were. When Ayisha didn't pick up, she tried Chandra instead.

"Where are you guys? I'm already at the park's bus stop," Smitha said as soon as Chandra answered.

"Well… we're still at the bazaar," Chandra replied hesitantly.

"What?" Smitha exclaimed with a mix of disbelief and frustration in her voice.

"We got so caught up in our spree that neither of us checked the time. Honestly, I wouldn't have even noticed if you hadn't called. Right now, Ayisha is in the dressing room trying on various outfits," Chandra explained.

"Wow! How much did you buy to lose track of time?" Smitha asked incredulously.

"*Nothing!* We bought *nothing*. But it was nice to look around!" Chandra responded. After a brief pause, she added, "How about we join you there in a bit? Can you wait? We'll leave right away." Her voice carried the unmistakable weight of guilt.

"No, that wouldn't work," Smitha said firmly. "It is already close to 5 p.m. The sunset is around 6, and the park closes at 7. It doesn't make sense to start from the bazaar now. Just finish your shopping and then give me a call. We'll decide from there, depending on the time."

"Oh, okay. And… I'm really sorry about this. You're all alone again," Chandra apologised.

"That's all right, don't worry about it. I'll get going now." Smitha replied before ending the call. She glanced at her phone's blank screen and let out an audible sigh, feeling a wave of disappointment wash over her. After a moment, she took a deep breath and muttered,

"Let's go," pushing away the sadness. She began walking toward the park with a faint smile that didn't quite reach her eyes.

CHAPTER 2

The park was just a short walk from the bus stop. Its entrance was a large red gate that stood wide open, welcoming visitors. A member of the park staff, dressed in white, greeted her with a friendly smile. Smitha smiled back and gave a slight nod in acknowledgement.

The park was even more beautiful than she had imagined. At its centre stood the funhouse, a vibrant and colourful building that commanded attention. A pathway cutting through a well-maintained lawn led directly to it. The path was paved with brightly coloured stones and lined with bushes dotted with vivid, colourful flowers, alternating with the most striking pink bougainvillaea trees Smitha had ever seen. Further along, a few coconut trees swayed gently in the breeze. The bold colours of the path and light green grass created a stunning contrast against the backdrop of the dark, dense forest in the distance.

It was a busy Friday evening. Children ran about in excitement, with parents trailing behind, wearing weary but content smiles. Shrieks of laughter and lively chatter blended with the music from the funhouse, filling the air with energy. Near the building, the pathway widened into a circular loop, lined with vendors selling balloons and toys for the eager kids.

Smitha walked slowly towards the funhouse, taking in the world around her with each step. She felt like Dorothy from The Wizard of Oz, only this time, she was following a colourful path instead of the yellow brick road.

The funhouse was a circular building painted in bright yellow, adorned with blue doors and windows. Speckles of red and orange polka dots decorated the exterior, resembling a whimsical carnival. It featured three floors, including the ground floor, and a circular balcony wrapped around each level. It was crowded with families enjoying the view of the park. The entrance boasted a giant blue double door painted onto the wall. Two smaller human-sized single doors served as entrance and exit points. These doors were also bright blue, blending seamlessly with the vibrant design of the larger door.

The entrance to the building had a slow-moving queue. A wooden plaque reading *Ticket Counter* pointed to the right, where a small hut stood. Its comically pointed roof, adorned with polka dot décor, perfectly matched the park's playful theme.

Smitha purchased her ticket and took her place in the queue, waiting to be let in. The line moved slowly, but soon enough, it was her turn. As she stepped inside the fun house, she felt a surge of excitement. The inside of the funhouse was as colourful as the outside. It featured a series of fun attractions that led to a staircase at the end that Smitha could take to the next floor. She could also bypass them and head straight up the stairs. Some parents who didn't want to join their children opted for that route.

Smitha felt like she was the only adult without an accompanying child in the room, but she didn't mind it.

Visiting such carnival-like places had been a rare event in her childhood, and she was determined to relish every moment.

The entrance led her to a vibrant floor, where a clear path directed her onward. Following the brightly painted arrows, she ventured across a series of colourful bridges, each one presenting its own unique challenge. The first bridge featured free-rotating sections that made walking a delightful test of her balance. The second, a slightly elevated rope bridge, swayed beneath her feet, the wobbly platforms adding an element of thrill.

With each careful step, Smitha's concentration sharpened. She focused solely on maintaining her footing. After successfully crossing each bridge, a cheerful electronic voice congratulated her, filling her with a sense of achievement.

Next came the third and final bridge, an animated glass structure that created the illusion of standing above turbulent waters. As the wind gusted from hidden vents and sound effects echoed around her, the experience felt incredibly immersive. Halfway across, a sudden crack made her heart race. She looked down only to see a tiny fracture forming in the glass beneath her. With her next step, the shattering sound of breaking glass reverberated through the air, heightening the moment's intensity.

Once she crossed the bridge, the path led her along the walls of the fun house, where mirrors distorted her reflection in playful and comical ways. As she continued, colourful lights danced from the ceiling, casting a lively glow over the space.

With her senses tingling, Smitha took the stairs to the first floor. This level offered a different atmosphere, with ample open space inviting everyone to explore freely. Spinning floors playfully altered her direction at every turn, adding an unexpected twist to her adventure. The walls were adorned with Minion-themed decorations, their bright yellow figures sporting oversized glasses, creating a cheerful ambience.

One section caught her attention: a musical instrument floor where each tile produced a distinct note. Drawn to the piano tiles—the only ones unoccupied by children—Smitha couldn't resist. She eagerly tapped on them, relishing the delightful melodies that filled the air and added to the fun house's enchanting atmosphere.

Smitha was having so much fun that she didn't notice how quickly time had passed. It wasn't until she saw the light dimming through one of the windows that she glanced at her watch. It was 5:45 PM, and the sun was set to go down at 6. Realising she didn't have much time, she stopped playing with the piano tiles and made her way towards the terrace.

While taking the stairs, she passed through the second floor, pausing momentarily to take in her surroundings. This floor was just as lively as the others, with spring-loaded platforms that bounced up and down with every step. Each bounce triggered a burst of flashing colours, delighting both kids and adults alike. The energy in the room was infectious, but after a long look, Smitha reminded herself of the time and continued her journey to the terrace.

At the top of the stairs stood a man in uniform. "Good evening, Ma'am. I hope you've had a fun time," he greeted her with a polite smile.

"Yes, I did. Thank you for asking," Smitha replied, reaching for the door to the terrace.

Before she could open it, the man spoke again. "Once you enter the gallery, you won't be able to return to the fun house. Would that be all right, Ma'am?"

Smitha nodded, "Yes, that's fine."

"In that case, may I see your ticket?" he asked, extending his hand.

She handed him the ticket. He carefully punched a hole in it and pushed the door open. "Thank you. Enjoy the sunset," he said, flashing a warm smile.

Smitha returned the smile and stepped out onto the terrace.

As Smitha stepped onto the terrace, she first noticed the yellowing sky—an unmistakable sign that sunset was fast approaching. She glanced around, taking in the view and searching for the perfect spot to settle down.

The terrace was more than just an ordinary rooftop. It seamlessly merged with the hilltop beyond, expanding into a vast open space that stretched out before her. "Terrace" no longer seemed fitting to describe such an expansive area. The building was perched on the sharp edge of a cliff, carefully designed to leave the gentle, sloping side of the hill and its dark, emerald-green forest untouched. The contrast of the forest-covered western slopes and the sheer cliff overlooking the calm ocean made this location a visitor's favourite.

The terrace hosted a vibrant gallery with benches painted in a spectrum of colours, all strategically positioned to offer perfect sunrise and sunset views. A fence formed a neat circle around the edge, preventing any adventurous souls from wandering too close to the dangerously steep slopes just beyond.

To the left of the gallery, the bright yellow canteen walls drew Smitha's attention. Next to its counter was a chalkboard listing the day's specials in neat handwriting. The full menu was printed and displayed above the counter. Behind the counter stood a man in a white apron, calling out bill numbers as he slid plastic trays of food through the serving window. The hum of the canteen added a lively backdrop to the tranquil atmosphere.

Smitha glanced at the colourful benches once more. She realised that if she sat there, the sunset view would be perfect—peaceful and uninterrupted.

Before settling down on one of the benches, she walked toward the fence, eager to take in the view. Beyond the fence lay a vast green carpet that stretched before her, the terrain uneven with small hills rising and falling. Their soft contours blended into the distance. The setting sun cast long shadows across the far-off hills, making them appear larger than they truly were. The trees draping the hill beneath her sparkled in the fading light, their lime-green leaves gleaming like peridot gems.

Mesmerised by the scene, Smitha focused intently, wanting to capture every detail and etch the image in her memory. The rolling hills, the shimmering trees— everything seemed perfect. But as her gaze wandered, she noticed something unusual. In the far-right corner of her view, a grey speck stood out against the vibrant green, like a coffee stain on a white shirt. Squinting, she realised it was a stone structure—a small temple tower, or gopuram. Likely an old shrine tucked away in the landscape.

Intrigued by the sight, she lingered for a moment before returning her focus to the breathtaking view, the vibrant greenery now permanently etched in her mind.

Smitha slowly made her way to the nearest bench without taking her eyes off the view. Settling in comfortably, she watched as the sun inched closer to the horizon. It seemed to descend in mere moments. As darkness crept across the sky, the soft yellow glow deepened into a bright orange, then a fiery blood-red, before fading into a rich purple. Finally, the darkness swallowed the sky completely, leaving only the faintest traces of the day that had just passed.

The sudden chill in the air nudged Smitha out of her reverie. Realising it had been hours since she last ate, she decided that it was time to grab something warm. At the canteen, Smitha glanced at the day's special—**Cheese Maggi** was scrawled in chalk on the board. *'It's been a year since I last had Maggi,'* she thought with a nostalgic smile. As she approached the billing counter, she checked the prices of the items. To her surprise, even a bottle of water was priced at ₹100, and the Maggi was ₹300. *'I could buy a packet for ₹15. There's no way I'm paying that,'* she thought, shaking her head. She was unwilling to spend so much on such a simple dish, so she decided to eat elsewhere.

'*I still have time till 7*,' she mused, deciding to sit a bit longer. She found a nearby bench and sat down facing the sea. The moonlight cast a serene glow over the water. Settling in, she pulled out her phone and put on her headphones, ready to enjoy some music under the moonlit sky. But as soon as she unlocked her phone, she noticed four missed calls—two from Ayisha and two from Chandra—along with several messages.

Concerned, she quickly called them back even before reading the messages.

"Hello," Smitha said as soon as the call connected.

"Hi! What happened? We've been trying to reach you for the last hour," Ayisha's voice came through, sounding concerned.

"I put my phone on silent. I didn't want to be distracted by work calls."

"Oh... I figured that might be it. That's why I sent you those messages."

"I didn't get a chance to read them yet. I called you as soon as I saw the missed calls."

"No worries. We're leaving the bazaar now. Are you done with the park, or do you need more time?"

"I'm all done here."

"Great. Do you want to meet back at the room?" Ayisha quickly suggested.

"I'm starving, actually. How about we meet at Taffles restaurant??"

"That's a bit out of the way for us—it doesn't fall on our bus route," Ayisha paused, and Smitha could hear her and Chandra mumbling in the background. "How about Lavonne Café? It's a good place and a decent halfway point."

"Sounds good! I'll try to catch the 6:30 bus. If I'm on time, I should be there by 6:50. I'll text you once I'm on the bus."

"Perfect. We'll head out too. See you there, bye!" Ayisha said, ending the call.

Smitha glanced at the time and quickly hurried towards the bus stop.

The Island of Virdona

CHAPTER 3

The three friends sat comfortably at a corner table in Lavonna Café, the warm inviting ambience enveloping them like a soft blanket. With their plates half-empty and stomachs pleasantly full, they leaned back into the plush rustic chairs, feeling the day's weariness melt away. The gentle flicker of candlelight on their table and the quiet murmur of the café set the perfect backdrop for their relaxed conversation as they basked in the comforting glow of both the space and each other's company.

"*Nothing?* How do you return empty-handed after spending an entire day at the bazaar?" Smitha asked Ayisha with disbelief.

"You know me! This shouldn't be a surprise," Ayisha replied with a shrug.

"I'm never going on another shopping spree with you," Chandra chimed in, pointing at Ayisha in playful banter. "I've exhausted all my energy. I can't wait to sink into my soft bed."

"That's classic Ayisha!" she proclaimed with pride. "But enough about me, Smitha—how was your day?"

"Every moment was something to remember. We should definitely go back for the sunset sometime. Though, I doubt you two would enjoy the funhouse."

"Oh, was the viewpoint that good?" Ayisha asked, intrigued.

"Good? That's an understatement! The emerald green forest shimmered under the golden hues of the sunset," Smitha said, mimicking a dreamy gaze, trying to sound poetic.

"Oh my God, she's turned into a poet! We have to check it out now," Chandra teased, laughing.

"It was stunning," Smitha agreed before adding with a sigh, "But their canteen prices were ridiculous. They were charging ₹300 for Maggi. I couldn't bring myself to buy it," she said, casting a wistful glance at one of the empty plates. "It's been over a year since I last had Maggi."

"That's the price you pay for the view, not the food," Chandra reasoned. "But hey, we can go now if you want." She looked at Ayisha, checking if she was on board with the idea.

"Why not? The night is young," Ayisha chimed in, her eyes lighting up with excitement.

Smitha, though tempted, looked concerned, "The park gates would've been closed by now. I saw the staff preparing to lock it up, and I'm pretty sure the canteen's closed too."

"No, no," Ayisha waved off the concern. "I heard the canteen is so popular that they keep the back gate open just to access it. You can't get into the main park from there, but you can still reach the canteen."

Smitha frowned, "I really doubt that. I didn't see any other way to the canteen. The only entrance was through the building, and everyone was packing up when I left."

Ayisha remained insistent. "Trust me, the canteen is a big deal! Imagine having dinner there if the viewpoint is as stunning as you said! That's probably why the prices are high and why it's so popular."

"Are you sure?" Smitha asked, still not fully convinced.

"Ayisha is *never* wrong," she declared with a playful grin. She was speaking about herself in the third person once again.

Chandra, eager to persuade, jumped in. "Why don't we just go? The buses run there until midnight. Worst case, we waste a couple of hours, but at least we'll get a scenic ocean-view ride at night."

Smitha hesitated momentarily, but the thought of a moonlit ride along the ocean—and, most importantly, the irresistible lure of Maggi—began to sway her. With a smile, Smitha finally relented, "Alright, let's go."

***

The three of them made their way to the bus stop, eager to get on their way. The night air had grown still and quiet, with the only sound being the distant hum of a passing vehicle. The area around Lavonna Café, located on the outskirts of town, felt almost deserted at this hour, adding to the serene atmosphere.

"How long do we need to wait?" Ayisha asked, her impatience creeping in.

"Just a little while. There's a bus every half hour until midnight, and it's almost 8:15," Smitha reassured while glancing at her phone.

"Wait, 8 PM? Will we even make it to the canteen before it closes?" Chandra asked, a hint of worry dawning on her.

"Don't worry, it only takes about 15 minutes to get there," Smitha replied confidently, speaking from experience.

"Okay," Chandra responded with a small sigh of relief, though still uncertain.

A few minutes passed in silence, with each scrolling through their phones to pass the time. The street around them was quiet, the occasional distant sound of a car being the only noise.

"How much longer?" Ayisha asked again. "It's past 8:15."

"Relax, it's probably just a couple of minutes late," Smitha said, her voice calm. "Why are you so restless?"

Ayisha shuffled a little closer and lowered her voice. "Look around. There's only one other person here." She discreetly pointed towards a middle-aged man sitting alone at the other end of the stop. "It feels... strange."

"You're just used to the constant noise of the city," Chandra chimed in with a knowing smile. "Towns like this start winding down around 9 PM. That's why it feels so empty."

Ayisha let out a soft sigh, still not entirely comforted. "Okay, if you say so."

Soon, the bus arrived, its headlights cutting through the dimly lit street. They boarded swiftly, noticing how sparsely filled it was, with just a few passengers scattered across the seats. They found a row on the ocean side where they could sit together, eager to take in the view.

As the bus cruised along the coastal road, the night breeze carrying the scent of the sea grew stronger. However, the view was far from what they had imagined. Instead of a sparkling ocean, there was an endless inky void. Streaks of white broke the darkness where the moonlight caught the tips of crashing waves. It was hauntingly beautiful, and the rhythmic sound of the waves against the shore added a sense of calm to their journey.

One by one, the few remaining passengers disembarked until the three friends were the only ones left after the last but one stop.

"These parts of the island aren't frequented by people at this hour. Are you girls sure you'll be safe at the next stop?" asked the conductor, who was a well-aged man with a kind face. His tone carried a genuine concern.

Not wanting to delve too deeply into their plans, Chandra took the lead. "Yes, we're joining a larger group near the park entrance. From there, we're planning to observe the tides of the ocean. We'll be back soon."

"Students, huh? I've heard there are plenty of activities happening on the island. It's refreshing to see young people taking an interest in nature," the conductor replied, his tone friendly and warm.

The three girls exchanged awkward but polite smiles, nodding in agreement.

The bus soon came to a halt at their destination. As they stepped off one by one, the conductor called out,

"Stay safe!" His kind words lingered in the air as the bus pulled away, leaving the girls standing in the quiet night.

"Why does this place look so abandoned?" Smitha asked, her nervousness creeping in.

There was a pause as Ayisha and Chandra looked around, both observing the desolate surroundings for signs of activity.

"Ayisha, where did you hear that the canteen was popular? I don't think that's the case," Smitha pressed, scanning the area.

"There's no one around. Not even stray vehicles," Chandra added, frowning as she surveyed the dimly lit street.

"I saw it in an Instagram reel. It looked really lively in the video," Ayisha explained, her voice faltering slightly.

Smitha closed her eyes and let out a deep sigh. "I guess the Instagrammer exaggerated. They probably filmed it close to the 7 PM closing time, when the darkness would have already set in."

"Since we're already here, why don't we check if the gates are open? There's no point in speculating," Chandra suggested, attempting to lighten the mood.

"Right, we're already here," Ayisha chimed in, trying to sound optimistic.

"Alright, let's make haste. I don't want to linger any longer than necessary," Smitha said, keeping her concern under wraps. After all, the park bordered the Tavora Forest, and friendly crowds were unlikely to pass by at this hour. There had been stories of wild animals roaming the area when human activity dwindled.

The three of them crossed the road and walked towards the park. The front entrance was well-placed and easily accessible from the main road, allowing them to spot it even in the dim light.

"Do you know how to get to the back gate?" Smitha asked Ayisha.

"Not exactly. As we walk toward the main gate, there should be a small turn that takes us around the fenced area of the park to the back entrance," Ayisha replied.

"Oh, okay," Smitha said, nodding.

"Since the main entrance is right here, why don't we ask the security for directions? It would be terrible if we got lost," Chandra suggested.

"Sure," Smitha agreed with a smile. *'She always tries to bring out the best in every situation,'* she thought. Although she was best friends with Ayisha, they never looked eye to eye on many things. On the other hand, Chandra was the perfect middle woman who helped bridge the gap between their differing viewpoints.

They started their walk towards the gate. The cool wind of the starry night blowing across their faces created a serene atmosphere. The tranquil environment magically calmed their nerves. The short walk led them to the park entrance, which was now closed. It was locked with a giant red lock that matched the size of the enormous red gate.

"Looks like there's no one around," Smitha remarked, glancing around, hoping to spot someone.

Chandra stepped closer to the gate to get a better look at the park. "Nope. There's definitely no one here," she said. She turned back to the others and asked, "Now what?"

"We saw a small turn back there, right? That should lead us to the back road," Ayisha insisted, tapping her phone screen to pull up a map. "See, it shows a road leading that way."

"Well, we have some time until the next bus arrives. Why don't we explore instead of waiting at the bus stop?" Chandra suggested, noticing the concern etched on Smitha's face. "The buses are usually on time, right?"

"Yes, the buses are punctual. But I'm telling you, at the first sight of a wild animal, I'm out of here. And... I won't hesitate to push you both down to gain a tactical advantage," Smitha replied, half-joking.

"We know," Ayisha and Chandra said in unison. The three of them shared a knowing look and then burst into laughter as they realised just how well they understood each other.

The three friends began to follow the path backwards, turning into the small alley that was meant to lead them to the back gate. The road curved along the perimeter of the park. It was a narrow lane barely wide enough for a car to squeeze through. The left side was lined with a fence that enclosed the park's manicured lawn, while the right side was lined with the evergreen trees of the Tavora forest. The leaves rustled playfully in the wind, and the crickets chirped rhythmically, creating a serene melody that filled the quiet darkness. Even though the moon was a few days shy of full, the moonlight illuminated the path like a soft torch, casting gentle shadows.

'Today has been one magical sight after another,' Smitha thought as she walked slowly, relishing every moment. The backdrop of the starry sky was a rare spectacle, and she could hardly tear her eyes away from the glittering stars. In that moment, all her earlier concerns faded into the background.

"Look at the road when you walk, not the skies. Don't trip and fall," Ayisha chimed in, her tone half-serious.

Smitha scrunched her eyebrows in annoyance. "Shhh... Don't talk. Let me enjoy the moment," she replied, her voice a mix of frustration and delight.

Amidst the lively chatter of the friends, they heard a peculiar rustling coming from one of the wild bushes. All three turned their heads to the source, where a stray dog emerged. It was a white dog with brown polka-dotted thin fur. Its expressive face lit up with joy at the sight of humans. The dog wagged its tail enthusiastically and trotted over to them.

"Aww, look at this handsome fellow coming towards us!" Chandra exclaimed, stepping forward slightly.

"Don't pet the dog, no matter how friendly it seems," Smitha cautioned, her scepticism kicking in.

"I won't," Chandra reassured her while bending down slightly to get a better look. "I don't have anything for you to eat, young fellow," she said, playfully addressing the dog.

As they continued their walk, the dog happily skipped alongside them, matching their pace. A contagious energy enveloped the group, and the tension of the evening began to melt away.

Soon, they spotted an open gate along the park fence. It was small and unassuming, lacking the grandeur of the main entrance.

"See! I wasn't wrong!" Ayisha proclaimed triumphantly.

"Yes, yes! Ayisha is the best!" Smitha chimed in, her tone playful. Chandra joined in, breaking into applause to further inflate Ayisha's ego.

As they neared the gate, Chandra noticed that the dog was no longer with them. She glanced back to see it standing a few meters away, looking a bit forlorn. *'I guess his territory ends there,'* she thought to herself, brushing off the feeling and walking ahead with her friends.

Chapter 4

The three friends stepped through the small, unassuming gate. Beyond it, the path led to a small clearing surrounded by thickening trees. Smitha, who had been admiring the scattered trees on the lawn, noticed how quickly the forest grew dense behind them. The clearing felt like a brief pause in the wall of greenery.

They moved forward, hoping to find someone who could point them toward the canteen. At the edge of the clearing stood a small, weathered cottage. Its wooden exterior showed signs of age, with moss creeping along the roof and faded paint hinting at better days. Outside, a middle-aged couple worked quietly, tending to simple chores. Their salt-and-pepper hair and easy movements spoke of years spent together in this peaceful spot.

The ladies slowed their steps, exchanging uncertain glances. They felt as if they had intruded on someone's private space as if this clearing belonged to another world entirely.

The couple looked up, their faces soft but tinged with surprise. They clearly hadn't expected visitors, especially this late. For a brief moment, no one spoke. The forest filled the silence, its quiet hum weaving through the stillness.

"Umm... the park is closed. And... this isn't the entrance to the park," said the woman, breaking the silence.

"I heard the park canteen is still open. Could you tell us how to get there?" Ayisha asked.

"No, the entire park is closed. You must have seen the locks on the front gates," the woman replied firmly.

"No, no, not the park—just the canteen," Ayisha insisted. "I heard it stays open until 9:30 and can be accessed from the back gate."

"Look, lady, there's no one here but us in the entire vicinity," the man cut in, his tone sharp with irritation. "Besides, what are you doing out here at this hour? You don't seem to belong here, and our house isn't some tourist stop," he added, clearly annoyed. His wife gently placed her hand on his arm, signalling him to calm down.

Before Ayisha could respond, Smitha quickly interjected, hoping to de-escalate the situation. "Oh, we're really sorry! If that's the case, we'll leave right away. We were just following the fence around the park and stumbled across this gate. We thought it was the back entrance—we didn't realise this was private property."

The woman, now calmer, replied, "Alright, it's just that we've never seen anyone wander back here, especially at this hour." She paused before continuing, "This area is part of the park, but it's accessible only to staff. We live here to take care of it full-time."

"The entire park? All by yourselves? Don't you get scared at night?" Chandra asked, wide-eyed, letting her curiosity get the best of her.

Both Smitha and Ayisha turned to look at her, a mixture of surprise and awkwardness flashing across their faces. *'This is neither the time nor place for such invasive questions,'* Smitha thought, inwardly cringing. *'Oh God, how do we excuse ourselves and leave?'*

The couple laughed gently. "Oh, don't worry about that. Our ancestors lived in these lands, and now we live here," the lady explained with a warm smile. "I know these forests like the back of my hand. Since we already lived here, the park authorities hired us to ensure no lost travellers wander too far into the woods."

"We're the lost travellers, aren't we?" Ayisha whispered, catching the subtle jab.

"I think so," Chandra whispered back, suppressing a grin.

"Thank you for your time. We'll be on our way now," Chandra said out loud, her voice polite. "We apologise once again for the intrusion."

They turned to leave, but suddenly, Smitha hesitated.

"W-Wait, umm... I saw a stone building. Is that also yours? It looked stunning," she blurted out, almost without thinking. A strange urgency welled inside her as though the question carried an unanticipated weight.

Her words froze them all in place. The couple exchanged glances, their expressions shifting from mild surprise to something more guarded—maybe even hostile.

The man spoke first, his voice edged with suspicion. "How did you see that place? You shouldn't be able to access it."

Smitha felt her pulse quicken. "No, I didn't go near it," she stammered. "I could get a glimpse of it from the hilltop.

"That shrine was built by our ancestors thousands of years ago," the man said, still guarded. "No one knows exactly when, but no one is allowed to go near it." His tone became more forceful. "It's a long story, too long for now. You girls don't go looking for trouble in the forest at night. Go back home."

"Yes, yes, we are going right away," said Chandra while tugging on Smitha's hand, gesturing her to leave.

Smitha, still curious, pointed toward a muddy trail leading into the dark forest. "Oh, does that pathway lead to the shrine? It seems to be in that direction."

The man's face darkened, his voice rising. "You—" he started, but the woman cut him off gently. "We won't give you any answers tonight. We don't want to tempt you into dangerous adventures. Go home. If you're still curious, come back tomorrow when the sun is up. I'll tell you what you want to know."

Sensing the rising tension, Chandra tugged harder on Smitha. "Definitely. Thank you for being so patient with us. We're leaving now," she said quickly.

"Ow! That's painful. I'm coming! I'm coming!" Smitha whispered angrily to Chandra, wincing as she was dragged along. Then she turned back to the couple, "We won't go into the forest. Thanks again. Have a good night."

The three friends hurried away, Chandra practically dragging Smitha behind her.

Clack.

The sound of a lock clicking shut echoed behind them as they left the gated area. "Stick to the road. There are many snakes in the shrubs," the woman's voice called out.

"Of course. Thank you for the warning!" Ayisha shouted as they hastened their pace.

***

Once they were well out of earshot from the couple, "What were you thinking?" Chandra snapped angrily at Smitha.

Smitha had rarely seen Chandra this angry. "I-I don't know. Curiosity got the better of me," she replied, her head drooping in guilt.

"And you—" Chandra turned towards Ayisha, her voice sharp. "Why are you going around asking personal questions to strangers we just met?"

"There's nothing wrong with being curious," Ayisha shot back defensively. "It's not like I said anything inappropriate," she added, lifting her chin slightly, subtly hinting at Smitha's earlier conversation.

Chandra cut them both off, clearly not in the mood for excuses. "Enough. Both of you walk faster. We need to catch the bus."

She marched ahead, her tone leaving no room for argument. "We're catching that bus and going straight home. I don't want to hear anything more from either of you."

Smitha and Ayisha followed her in silence. Slowly, the tense atmosphere began to fade into a calmer, more serene one.

CHAPTER 5

"Woof! Woof!"

As they walked further along the road, the friends heard a dog bark. The white stray dog was waiting for them at the curve ahead. Excited to see them, the dog jumped up and down, its tail wagging happily. They couldn't help but smile at the sight.

Chandra, already ahead, quickened her pace to close the distance between her and the dog. Reaching the dog, she got down on one knee and petted it excitedly. The other two caught up with her no sooner than a couple of minutes later. Just as they bent down to pet the dog, it ducked playfully and dashed ahead.

The dog stopped a few paces away, turning back to face them as if inviting them to follow.

Chandra, still crouched, turned to her friends with a playful grin. "You scared him away!" she teased. But her amusement quickly faded when she noticed their wide-eyed expressions. Both were staring past her with a mix of shock and dread.

"What's going on—" Chandra began, but her words caught in her throat as she turned to look. The sight before her stole the breath from her lungs.

The creature before her was no longer a stray dog. It had transformed into something much taller, a majestic being. The familiar brown polka dots had faded away, replaced by fur so long and luxurious that it cascaded down its body like a waterfall of silver-white strands. The once short, scruffy coat now radiated an otherworldly elegance, shimmering softly as though it was spun from moonlight itself.

A thick mane of white fur framed its face, denser than the rest of its body, reminiscent of a lion's mane but far more mystical, as if every strand held centuries of wisdom. Despite the gentle night breeze, the fur remained perfectly still. It was untouched by the wind—protected by some invisible barrier that separated this creature from the earthly world.

As the creature stretched its legs forward in a slow, graceful motion, an ethereal glow enveloped it. It was the kind of light that defied earthly colours. It was neither white nor blue nor yellow, but something in between, as if the moon had poured its essence into the being. It radiated a presence both calming and awe-inspiring. It felt as though it belonged to a realm beyond time and space.

But the most striking transformation lay in its eyes. Gone were the playful earthly eyes of a stray. In their place were deep endless black voids. These eyes seemed to hold the secrets of the universe, drawing in anyone who looked into them, making the observer feel small and insignificant in comparison. They weren't frightening but vast and infinite, as though staring into them could lead one to a different dimension.

The creature stood there, serene and powerful, bathed in its soft glow.

Soon, the angelic creature began to move towards the three friends. Its steps were slow and deliberate. With each stride, its paw prints left behind a faint, ethereal glow that shimmered briefly under the moonlight before fading into the earth. The air around them grew calm, and an almost sacred stillness settled in as though time itself had slowed. The three friends stood frozen in place, unable to look away from the creature as it approached.

The animal glided past Chandra and stopped in front of Smitha. Its presence was both gentle and commanding. Its void-like eyes were fixed on her, not with menace but with expectation. As if waiting for her to understand something profound. Smitha's heart pounded as she exchanged glances with her two friends. They remained entranced, their expressions locked in wonder. They hadn't yet grasped the significance of the moment.

Smitha instinctively extended her right hand without fully understanding why, palm facing upward, like a silent offering or plea. The creature lowered its majestic head and gently placed something onto her hand. It then took a step back as if giving her space to comprehend.

Smitha's gaze dropped to her palm. Whatever the creature had given her glowed so intensely that she couldn't discern its shape or form. The light radiated so brightly that it seemed to pulsate, casting soft rays around her hand, making the object feel weightless.

She squinted, trying to make sense of what she held, but the object's brilliance defied her attempts to focus. Whatever it was, it wasn't just a simple token. It was something far beyond her understanding.

Before Smitha could fully grasp the mysterious object in her hand, a sudden, powerful wind swept through, wrapping around her like an invisible force. The wind swirled around her as if she were in the eye of a storm. Its force was strong but harmless. Confusion gripped her as she looked around, trying to understand what was happening.

Just as quickly as it had come, the wind released her, rushing away as if it had a will of its own. But the scene in front of her left her heart pounding—both Ayisha and Chandra were now trapped within the same mysterious gust. The wind spiralled tightly around them. Their faces were etched with panic. They flailed helplessly, unable to escape the force that confined them, their arms reaching out in desperation.

"Ayisha! Chandra!" Smitha screamed, her voice cracking with urgency as she lunged toward Ayisha. Her hand stretched out, trying to grasp her friend's, but the wind was too fierce. It pushed her back, creating an impenetrable barrier between them. Smitha's outstretched fingers came frustratingly close, but the distance between them felt impossible to close.

"Ayisha, reach out to my hand!" Smitha yelled again, her voice strained. But Ayisha, trapped within the violent whirlwind, couldn't hear her. The wind drowned out her words, leaving only muffled cries in the air. Smitha watched in horror as Ayisha mouthed the word, 'Help,' her voice lost in the howling wind.

Fear surged through Smitha, her heart pounding as desperation gripped her. Frozen by the mysterious spectacle unravelling around her, she felt utterly helpless. Her eyes darted to the radiant white creature standing before her, still calm and otherworldly.

"Help," she cried out in anguish. Her voice was trembling as though the weight of the situation was too much to bear. Somehow, deep down, she knew this creature—this ethereal being—was at the centre of it all, connected to everything happening. It had to be the key to ending this chaos.

The creature's black, void-like eyes locked onto hers, a stillness in its gaze that both terrified and reassured her. For a moment, time seemed to freeze. Sitting the glowing object in her palm, Smitha waited, her breath held in the balance. '*Would this being who had started everything answer her call?*'

As if answering her plea, Smitha watched in awe as two more creatures emerged from the depths of the thick forest moments later. The first was a cat-like creature, its fur shimmering with an ethereal luminescence, a pristine white that seemed to absorb the moonlight around it. Its eyes pitch dark like a black hole at the centre of a shining star. It spoke of an intelligence that transcended the ordinary. The feline moved with a graceful fluidity, every step delicate yet purposeful, leaving behind a faint trail of glowing paw prints that flickered like the last remnants of a dying star.

The second creature was a magnificent bird, equally ethereal in its appearance. It was cloaked in white feathers that glowed softly, creating an almost celestial aura. Its outstretched wings revealed intricate patterns that seemed to shift and dance as it moved, reflecting the moon's gentle light. Its three long tail feathers were most striking, which flowed behind it like silken ribbons, each shimmering with iridescent hues that changed with every subtle movement. These feathers elongated into graceful spirals, reminiscent of comets streaking across the night sky, leaving trails of shimmering light in their wake.

Together, the feline and the bird created an enchanting tableau, an otherworldly presence that harmonised with the glowing hound at the forefront. Smitha's heart raced at the sight, sensing that these mystical beings were not just mere apparitions.

Smitha stared in awe as the feline moved gracefully toward Chandra. Its luminous paws glided effortlessly across the ground. It seemed to cut through the swirling, monstrous wind as if the storm meant nothing to it. Without hesitation, the feline rubbed its glowing head against Chandra's legs. In an instant, the violent gusts that surrounded her came to an abrupt halt as though they had been commanded to cease. A gentle, soothing purr emanated from the feline. This softened Chandra's tense posture. The calmness washed over her.

Meanwhile, the majestic bird glided effortlessly through the air, its wings barely disturbed by the chaotic vortex surrounding Ayisha. It flew straight into the eye of the whirlwind, undeterred by the violent forces that raged around her friend. With delicate precision, the bird landed on Ayisha's shoulder, its weight barely noticeable. At that very moment, the fierce winds that had imprisoned Ayisha fell silent. The air around her stilled, and a sense of serenity replaced the turmoil.

Both Chandra and Ayisha stood still, their breaths steadying as the mystical creatures brought them a peace that felt as otherworldly as the beings themselves.

The three exchanged glances, each overwhelmed by the surreal situation they found themselves in. They had a lot to say, yet nothing seemed to come out.

"..." Smitha opened her mouth as if to speak, but no words followed. Her thoughts were jumbled, unable to form a coherent sentence. She simply closed her mouth, returning to the puzzling silence.

"Well, say something!" Ayisha demanded, her bewildered expression only adding to the tension.

"Say what? You can start," Smitha shot back, still at a loss for words herself.

Chandra took a deep, audible breath. The sound cut through the lingering quiet like a sharp knife, instantly drawing the attention of the others. Smitha and Ayisha turned to her, waiting for her to break the silence.

"Now... what do we do?" Chandra asked, her voice steady but laced with uncertainty.

The others shook their heads, mirroring her confusion. No one had an answer. The world around them had shifted, and none of them knew how to make sense of it.

"Smitha, your hand... what's that?" Chandra asked, pointing towards Smitha's hand.

Smitha felt a strange warmth in her hand, suddenly realizing she was tightly clenching the object that had been handed to her. The light from the object pierced through the gaps between her fingers, casting beams of light as if she were holding a miniature torchlight. She barely noticed it until Chandra pointed it out.

Smitha raised her hand, slowly opening her fist to reveal the object. The others huddled closer, their breath catching as the bright glow subdued, revealing a shape. It was a key—an otherworldly key that still shimmered softly with a gentle, bioluminescent glow as though it had been bathed in algae. The smooth metal had an unearthly shine, its intricate design unlike anything they had ever seen.

Before they could make sense of it, Smitha felt something brush against her legs. She glanced down to see the softly glowing fur of the hound. It moved past her and headed towards the park's back gate. Her eyes followed the being as it trotted a few steps ahead.

The other two ethereal creatures—the feline and the bird—followed closely behind. The bird, though its wings were still, hovered effortlessly in the air, as if suspended by an invisible force.

Ahead, the path leading into the park seemed to light up on its own. Small, glowing orbs of light hovered just above the ground, illuminating the way with a subtle mystical glow. The entire scene was like something from another realm. It was a dreamlike passage stretching into the unknown.

The three beings paused and turned back, their eyes fixed on the three friends. It was clear they were beckoning them to follow. The silent invitation hung in the air, and the glowing path seemed to pulse softly, waiting for the three friends to make their choice.

"Should we follow them?" Smitha asked, her voice a mix of curiosity and uncertainty.

"Are you crazy?" Ayisha shot back, her eyes wide with disbelief. "Something weird is going on. We don't even know what those things are!"

"But think about it," Chandra cut in, siding with Smitha. "Maybe this is some kind of revelation... a message, or a sign. Something beyond us. It feels like a divine intervention." Her voice grew quieter as if she were convincing herself as much as the others. "I mean, look at them."

Smitha nodded in agreement. Her gaze locked on the glowing animals that stood still, patiently waiting. "I feel like... we're meant to follow them," she added.

Ayisha crossed her arms, still hesitant. She said, "This is crazy. We're in the middle of nowhere with glowing animals after a weird encounter with that couple. Do you really think this is safe?"

Chandra sighed, "I know it sounds bizarre, but doesn't it feel... right? It's not like they're attacking us or anything. They gave us a key, Ayisha. A key! How can we just walk away from that?"

Ayisha hesitated, glancing back and forth between her two friends and the glowing creatures. "I just don't want us to get hurt."

Smitha stepped closer to Ayisha, her tone softening. "Neither do we, but I don't think they're here to hurt us. What if this is fate? Many people have walked this path, but what's the probability that this was presented to us? Maybe this key is connected to something important. Besides, we're together."

Ayisha sighed deeply, clearly torn. She rubbed her temples before finally giving in. "Fine. But the moment anything feels off, we turn back."

Chandra smiled, relieved, "Deal."

The three friends exchanged looks, forming a silent pact. Together, they turned towards the glowing path, ready to follow the ethereal beings into the unknown.

CHAPTER 6

The otherworldly beings led the way—the hound guiding Smitha, the feline guiding Chandra, and the bird guiding Ayisha. The trio followed the celestial beings who took them back towards the park's back gate. Their path was illuminated softly under the moonlight. It was as though the stars themselves had come down to mark their way.

As they walked further, they came upon the park's gate, which was locked shut. The glowing path extended beyond the gate, inviting them deeper inside. Though not as comically oversized as the front entrance, the gate was still large and imposing, with a giant rusted lock holding it firmly shut.

"Well, the gate seems to be locked. What do we do?" Ayisha asked, her voice laced with uncertainty as she eyed the giant lock securing the gate.

However, Chandra seemed unfazed. "Let's see. Maybe the gate will magically open. The night's already given us more than a few miracles, hasn't it? I believe there's a lot more yet to come," she said, her tone brimming with curious excitement.

As they stepped closer to the gate, something remarkable happened—the lock began to glow gently as if awakening to their presence. Simultaneously, the key in Smitha's hand started to pulse with warmth. It grew hotter with each passing second. Smitha lifted the key and watched it in awe as its glow began to pulse in perfect sync with the lock's light. It was as though the key was calling out to her, telling her precisely what needed to be done.

The celestial hound, which had been guiding Smitha, picked up its pace. It trotted forward, reaching the centre of the gate first. It pointed its snout directly at the lock and then turned its deep black eyes toward Smitha, waiting expectantly. She understood the silent message.

With a deep breath, Smitha took a step forward. Chandra and Ayisha watched in anticipation. The celestial beings stood calmly in their glowing forms. Smitha hesitated for a moment, and then she inserted the key into the glowing lock. The key fit perfectly. She twisted it. With a soft *click*, the lock fell away, releasing the heavy iron gate.

She pushed it open just enough for them to slip through, one by one. The celestial hound entered first, gracefully slipping past the gate. Smitha followed, feeling a strange sense of destiny pulling her forward. Chandra and Ayisha exchanged a quick glance, then hurried in behind her.

"Should we lock the gates back?" Ayisha whispered, her eyes darting nervously between the gate, the cottage, and the quiet road behind them.

"Why?" Smitha asked, genuinely confused.

"Keep your voice down!" Ayisha hissed, glancing around as if expecting the old couple to appear out of the shadows. "We don't want them waking up and seeing the gate wide open. And we *definitely* don't want them thinking some thieves broke into the park."

"That's actually a good point," Chandra agreed, lowering her voice to match Ayisha's. "Better safe than sorry."

"Alright, I'll lock it back," Smitha said, stepping forward. The gate creaked softly as she swung it shut, and with a quick motion, she re-secured the heavy lock. It no longer glowed; its job was clearly done, but the key in her hand still held a faint, steady light.

'I guess the lock's magic has served its purpose,' Smitha thought, glancing down at the glowing key before clenching her fist tight over the key for safekeeping

Inside the park, the celestial beings led them down a muddy trail. The narrow path wound through the dense forest like a forgotten secret, disappearing into the heart of the wilderness. The pathway was faintly lit by an eerie glow that seemed otherworldly. Spectral will-o'-wisps floated alongside the trail, illuminating every leaf, vine, and stem in sharp, dreamlike clarity.

"Didn't the couple say this path leads to the shrine?" Smitha asked, her voice barely above a whisper as if speaking too loudly would break the spell.

"They didn't," Chandra corrected, her tone matter-of-fact. "You just assumed it did."

"Well, what *is* this shrine, anyway?" Ayisha asked, her curiosity piqued despite her lingering apprehension.

"That's what we're about to find out," Smitha replied with a small smile, a flicker of excitement crossing her face. Without another word, she stepped onto the magical path.

Chandra and Ayisha exchanged glances before following her lead. Their footsteps left dark, wet impressions on the otherwise ethereal pathway. Together, they ventured deeper into the wilderness.

The path eventually led them to a small clearing where a moss-covered stone wall stood. Though ancient and crumbling in places, it remained remarkably sturdy. The glowing trail followed alongside the wall, guiding them toward a visible gap ahead.

"This could be the shrine!" Smitha whispered excitedly, barely able to contain her anticipation.

Chandra squinted at the structure. "It does look like an old temple. But it doesn't seem that big," she said, as though confirming Smitha's assumption.

Ayisha, standing on her tiptoes, tried to peer over the weathered stones. "I can't see anything beyond this," she muttered in frustration. The wall was too tall, shrouding whatever lay behind it in mystery.

Smitha pointed toward the gap in the stone. "The path seems to lead through there. Let's see if we can get a better view from there."

With silence as the response, the three of them cautiously moved forward. They were drawn in by the intrigue of what might lie beyond the ancient barrier.

The path following the wall eventually turned toward a gap and ended there. The gap wasn't a random break in the wall but an intentional entrance, marked by a standalone arch leading to whatever lay beyond—perhaps the shrine. Beyond the entrance, a dark void loomed, an impenetrable blackness that seemed to consume the surrounding light.

Flanking the entrance were two tall and imposing statues of men, each about six feet in height. Time had withered their faces, leaving them featureless, yet the rest of their forms were strangely well-preserved, untouched by the moss that clung to the walls. They stood like sentinels, guarding the way forward, their stony silence adding to the eerie atmosphere.

The three spectral creatures had walked up to the threshold of the dark opening. The hound, the feline, and the bird—all stood there, waiting patiently near the entrance as if expecting the friends to command them to proceed.

Smitha, Chandra, and Ayisha exchanged uneasy glances, the weight of their next step hanging in the air.

"I guess backing out is no longer an option if we set foot inside," Smitha said, her voice carrying a nervous edge.

Chandra nodded. "It does feel like that," she agreed. "So, what do you think? Should we go in?"

Ayisha squinted, trying to peer into the black void beyond the entrance. "I can't see a thing in there. It's pitch dark," she said, with uncertainty written on her face. "One part of me feels drawn to this—like we've come too far to stop. But the other part... it's scary. What if we're walking into something we don't understand?"

Chandra took a deep breath. "We shouldn't go in until we're all sure," she said, her voice steady despite the tension. "Let's weigh it out—pros and cons."

Smitha crossed her arms, nodding thoughtfully. "Well, pros? We're already here. This whole experience has been out of this world—literally. The beings gave us a key, led us here... I mean, this could be a once-in-a-lifetime opportunity."

Chandra chimed in, "True, there is definitely something special about this place. We've followed the signs so far, and nothing has harmed us. The beings seem peaceful, almost protective."

Ayisha added, even though she heisted at first, "But the cons... We don't know what is inside. It's dark. And what if we can't come back? What if it's dangerous?"

Smitha nodded in agreement. "Not to mention, we're heading deeper into the forest. There could be wild animals, and old temples usually have bats, maybe even snakes. Both aren't exactly good news for us."

"That's true," Chandra conceded, "but haven't you noticed? The divine creatures have been protecting us this far. I don't think they would lead us into danger. I believe they're here to protect and guide us."

"Are you sure about that?" Ayisha asked, still unsure.

"Yes, think about how we have been treated so far. And, listen carefully." Chandra said, pausing to give the other two sometime. "You can hear frogs croaking and crickets chirping, right? But we haven't encountered a single one of them. Frogs are everywhere—trust me, even in my tiny backyard. Yet, here? Nothing."

Smitha and Ayisha took a moment to consider this. Smitha spoke up first, "That's true. We should've seen something by now, but we haven't."

Ayisha, still hesitant, asked, "What if this leads us to another world?"

"You mean, like a magical portal?" Smitha scoffed but then stopped mid-sentence as Ayisha raised her eyebrows. "Okay, fair point. At this stage, anything seems possible."

Ayisha shifted her weight, glancing at the glowing beings. "I think we should go. We've trusted this strange world so far, so why not take it a bit further? I don't think we're here by accident. Maybe it's fate."

"That's a good point," Smitha agreed, her resolve strengthening. She looked over at Chandra and said, "Well?"

Chandra closed her eyes and let out a deep sigh before opening them again. "Alright... let's do it. I guess this is the journey we're meant to take."

The three friends exchanged determined glances, a shared smile passing between them. Without another word, they turned toward the dark, mysterious entrance, ready to take the next step in their extraordinary adventure.

"Wait!" Smitha exclaimed, halting abruptly, much to the annoyance of the others.

"What now?" Chandra asked, exasperation creeping into her voice.

Smitha hesitated, unsure how to explain her gut feeling. "Well... we can't see the glowing lights inside the wall, right? What if... what if we're not supposed to see whatever's in there?"

Chandra's brow furrowed in confusion. "What do you mean? How are we supposed to go inside if we're not supposed to see it?"

"I mean... should we keep our eyes closed?" Smitha suggested hesitantly.

Ayisha responded with a mix of frustration and disbelief while still processing what Smitha said. "And how exactly do we walk into a completely unfamiliar place with our eyes closed? That's barely feasible in our own homes. The place we know every inch of—let alone an abandoned shrine in the middle of nowhere."

"I don't know, it just feels like we're about to see something we're not meant to. I can't explain it," Smitha said, her anxiety evident. Seeing the puzzled expressions on Chandra and Ayisha's faces, she quickly added, "How about this? I'll close my eyes and keep my hand on one of your shoulders to guide me. Just in case."

Chandra and Ayisha exchanged looks, clearly unsure but unwilling to ignore Smitha's statement.

Ayisha sighed, "If you really feel that strongly about it... I suppose there's nothing we can do but go along."

Chandra nodded, though she still seemed doubtful. "Alright, Smitha. But stay close. This is weird enough without us getting separated."

Smitha gave a nervous smile, grateful for her friends' understanding. "Give me a minute," she said as she pulled her bag in front of her and rummaged through it. After a moment, she pulled out a shawl—the one she had used earlier to shield herself from the harsh sun. With a determined look, she folded it and tied it around her eyes like a blindfold. "Now I'm ready."

Chandra walked up to Smitha and gently placed her hand on her own. She looked at Ayisha, who seemed a bit sceptical but nodded. She then looked at the celestial creatures, who were standing patiently near the entrance. "I guess we're ready now," Chandra said, her voice steady but filled with anticipation.

As if responding to their resolve, the celestial beings moved forward, their glowing light now extending deeper into the dark void of the Shrine's entrance. The previously invisible pathway became visible, forming itself out of the darkness and leading further into the unknown.

Together, the three friends stepped forward. The celestial beings guided them as they crossed the threshold of the shrine walls. Their footsteps echoed faintly against the stone floor, and the air around them seemed to hum with a strange, ancient energy. Smitha, blindfolded and relying on her friends for guidance, could feel the palpable shift in the atmosphere. It was as though they had entered a different realm.

CHAPTER 7

Smitha felt an intense discomfort as soon as she blindfolded herself. The overwhelming pitch blackness was almost unbearable. Her other senses were heightened—the distant croaking of frogs, the cool air brushing against her skin, the faint hum in the atmosphere. However, the darkness was suffocating. A creeping sense of fear gnawed at her nerves. *'I can always take it off if everything seems alright,'* she reminded herself, trying to soothe her spiralling thoughts. Through the tension, she managed to say, "Now, I'm ready."

A sense of relief washed over her when she felt Chandra's hand reach out, steadying her in the void. This small gesture felt like a lifeline, tethering her to reality at that moment. Together, they took a few tentative steps forward, moving in what seemed like the direction of the shrine.

Then, something miraculous happened. When Chandra softly uttered, "I guess we're ready now," Smitha sensed a shift. Though her eyes were tightly closed, glowing lights began to seep through the darkness in her mind. At first, it was a gentle glow, but it quickly intensified, forming a clear pathway in her mind's eye. The path was etched into the void as though beckoning her forward, guiding her despite her blindness.

'So, this must be the path we're meant to take,' Smitha thought, feeling both amazed and unsettled. Several thoughts crowded her mind. *'How could I see the glowing*

path when my eyes were closed? Was this some kind of vision, or was it a manifestation of the magic surrounding them?'

Chandra, who wasn't blindfolded, continued to lead Smitha forward with confident steps. Even though Smitha could only see the glowing path in her mind, Chandra seemed to follow it perfectly. It was as if Chandra could see the trail in Smitha's mind. Smitha couldn't help but marvel at how seamlessly their movements aligned. Chandra's steady guidance felt like a natural extension of the vision Smitha was experiencing. It was as though celestial beings led Chandra down the same path that Smitha could sense despite her blindness.

Within moments of walking, Smitha felt a distinct shift in the atmosphere—a presence that made her skin prickle with awareness. The air grew heavier, not with danger, but with something ancient and powerful. It was as though they were crossing into a different realm altogether.

"Did we cross the archway?" Smitha asked, her voice betraying the nervous energy she felt.

"Yes, just now. Can you also feel it?" Chandra responded with her tone hushed.

Smitha nodded. "I can. The air feels... different." The change wasn't just in the atmosphere, "Everything around me feels altered. I feel that my senses have become sharper, as though the world has come into focus."

"Even though you are blindfolded?" Chandra asked sceptically.

"Yes, even though I am blindfolded," Smitha replied.

For Smitha, the glowing pathway ahead appeared more distinct now, its luminescence vivid in her mind. The celestial beings glided alongside the path, their figures crystal clear in a way that defied logic. Outside the path, she noticed faint reflections—objects in the darkness that caught the light and shimmered for a moment before disappearing into the shadows.

Curious and confused, Smitha asked the others, "What are you seeing?"

Ayisha responded first. "It's a small temple... though it doesn't look as abandoned as I thought it would be. It looks ancient, but someone has been taking care of it."

"How do you mean?" Smitha asked, intrigued.

Ayisha paused, considering. "Maybe that couple we met has been maintaining it?"

"I didn't mean that," Smitha said, tugging at her blindfold slightly. "I mean, how does it look? Remember, I'm blindfolded. Also, is the pathway still lit up?"

"It's not lit up like streetlights lighting up a road," Ayisha replied. "But yes, glowing spirits have lit up the pathway. The shrine's paved pathway is glowing like it did on our way here."

Chandra continued, "The glowing pathway is guiding us right into the temple. However, it is a small temple. You're right about it being old, but weirdly... it's almost as if time hasn't completely ruined it. The outside stone walls enclose a small shrine with two large, heavy doors sealing it shut. It definitely looks ancient, but somehow, it's still intact."

"And the statues?" Smitha pressed, trying to piece the scene together in her mind.

"The statues outside must be Yakshan—protectors, guarding whatever's inside the shrine," Chandra continued. "There are two more inside, one on each side of the heavy wooden doors. They look just like the ones we saw earlier, tall, imposing, and standing watch."

Chandra hesitated momentarily before adding, "But there's something strange here..."

Smitha tilted her head, sensing her friend's unease. "What do you mean by strange?"

"There are heads, just heads, of three statues on the side of the path. They're mounted on some sort of platform," Chandra said, her voice carrying a note of confusion.

"Heads?" Smitha asked, surprised. The thought of decapitated statues placed deliberately on a platform sounded unsettling.

"Yes, stone heads," Ayisha chimed in this time. "And they're all different. Each one looks like it belongs to a different person or being."

Smitha, curious but still blindfolded, asked, "Can you describe them? And maybe help me figure out where everything is? I need to understand the direction."

Chandra took a moment to respond, mentally mapping it out for Smitha. "Okay, directly in front of you, about four or five meters away, is the entrance to the small shrine. The path leads there straight from where we're standing—no twists, no turns. Now, toward your right, about two o'clock, there's one of the heads. I can't make out much detail, but it's definitely a person's head."

At this, Ayisha gently moved Smitha's hand to point towards the direction she was describing. "Here," she said, guiding her, "that's where it is."

Smitha stood still for a moment, allowing herself to focus. Though she couldn't physically see the statue, she felt its presence. It was vivid and unsettling, like it existed in her mind's glowing reflections. Even though the specifics of the statue remained unclear, she could sense it was something ancient and significant, like it was watching them from the side of the path.

"I can feel it," Smitha murmured, her tone soft but serious. "I don't know what it is, but its presence is... strong."

"Yeah," Chandra agreed quietly, her eyes still on the statues. "There's definitely something strange about this place."

"And toward your left, there are two more heads," Chandra pointed out, her voice carrying a hint of curiosity. "That's odd... Let's get closer to see them better."

The trio moved cautiously toward the first platform. As they neared it, Chandra stopped and peered at it momentarily before speaking. "It's the head of a Buddha," she said, her voice now quieter. "It's directly to your left... Don't touch it," she quickly added, noticing Smitha instinctively reach out.

"So, this must be a Buddhist shrine?" Smitha asked, her tone inquisitive.

"I'm not sure," Ayisha said with a slight shrug, her eyes scanning the surroundings as though seeking more clues. "It's not clear yet. Let's check the next statue."

They continued a few steps further to the next head, this one more elaborate. "This one's different," Chandra said, her brow furrowing. "It looks like a deity or a king. The face has a massive crown, intricately carved."

Smitha, whose vision picked up faint outlines through her blindfold, asked, "Does it have big circular earrings?"

Chandra and Ayisha exchanged glances.

"How did you know that?" Ayisha asked, her voice tinged with surprise.

Smitha hesitated for a moment. "I... I don't know. I can't see clearly, but I can almost see everything—just faint shapes, like an outline in my head. I can see the floating wisps lighting our path and the edges of where the light falls. Beyond that, though... it's all pitch black."

"Wow! Why did you wait so long to tell us something this important?" Ayisha asked, her voice tinged with both surprise and concern.

"I thought I was hallucinating," Smitha replied defensively, her tone softening as she continued. "That's why I asked for such a detailed description earlier. But... don't let go of me. I'm still terrified since I can't see either of you."

"I won't. Don't worry," Chandra reassured her, tightening her grip on Smitha's shoulder. "We'll stay together. Let's head towards the wooden doors."

As they moved forward, the eerie glow of the will-o'-wisps flickered, illuminating just enough to guide them but still leaving the shadows thick and foreboding. Smitha's heart raced as she followed Chandra's lead. Her heightened senses made every step feel heavier and the air denser.

As they neared the shrine's entrance, Smitha's vision suddenly burst with light, a vivid flash illuminating her mind. A new object materialised at the end of the path—an entrance, closed off by what appeared to be heavy wooden doors.

"Wow! Did you see that?" Ayisha exclaimed.

"See what? Did the doors open?" Smitha asked, her heart racing, eager to know what was happening.

"No, the doors are still closed, but they've started glowing brightly. The hound walked up to the front and touched the door. The moment it did, the whole entrance lit up. They look like ancient, heavy wooden doors," Ayisha explained, her voice filled with awe.

"And guess what?" Chandra added excitedly. "One of the doors has a keyhole. And surprise, surprise—the key in your hand is pulsating again!"

Smitha noticed the familiar warmth spreading through her palm. The key in her hand seemed to throb with life, much like before. She couldn't help but smile. "Looks like it's time. Let's go."

With Chandra guiding her, they walked toward the glowing doors, Ayisha following close behind. As before, the animals moved aside, respectfully stepping back to let them take the lead. Smitha felt for the keyhole, her hands trembling slightly as she slid the key in.

Clack.

The lock turned smoothly as if it had been recently oiled, untouched by the passage of time. But when she pushed against the doors, they didn't budge.

"The doors aren't moving. Can you help me?" Smitha called out in frustration.

The three women pressed their shoulders against the massive doors, pushing with all their combined strength. The rusty hinges groaned under the pressure. At first, the doors resisted stubbornly. But then, with a loud and reluctant creak, they swung open violently, flinging the trio inside.

Bang!

The sound of the heavy doors slamming against the stone walls reverberated through the tiny shrine, sending echoes that bounced around them like an ancient alarm. The sudden silence that followed felt thick with anticipation, as if the shrine had awoken from a deep slumber.

"Wow, that was loud," Smitha exclaimed, her voice echoing softly in the now eerily silent space. "What does it look like inside? I think it's smaller in here... and stuffier too," she added, still relying on the faint outlines she could see in her mind. She was eager to learn more, her excitement building despite the strange atmosphere.

Silence.

"Guys?" she called out, her voice quivering just a little. "Are you able to hear me?"

No response.

Smitha's heart began to race. She turned her head, straining to hear something—*anything*—but the quietness inside the shrine was absolute.

"Chandra? Ayisha?" she called out again, panic creeping in now. Her hands reached out, hoping to feel one of them nearby. Her breath quickened as the stillness became unbearable.

Her voice trembled, "Where are you?"

The only answer was the echo of her words as if the shrine was mocking her isolation.

CHAPTER 8

Smitha's mind swirled with panic and fear. After forcibly entering the shrine, her friends stopped responding. No matter how many times she called out, there was no answer. She was completely alone, trembling, her thoughts scattered by the shock of the situation.

Unsavoury thoughts flooded her mind. *'What happened to them? Are they hurt? Is there someone—or something else in the room with her? Or worse... am I in a different dimension? Could they be safe while she had fallen into a pit of nothingness?'*

Slap! She clapped her cheeks, snapping herself back to reality. Her pulse raced, but her mind cleared enough to think logically again.

She began to analyse the situation, considering the possibilities:

'If it's my friends who are in danger, and I'm the only one who's safe, then it must have to do with the blindfold. So, I shouldn't take it off.'

'If I fell into another world or unconsciousness, there's no point in removing it—better to keep it on.'

'If we're all trapped in different dimensions, taking the blindfold off might increase my chance of survival.'

'But if I'd been teleported somewhere dangerous, it would have already happened long before. I'm probably still in the same location. I'll keep the blindfold on.'

Smitha decided firmly, her resolve hardening with each thought.

She thrust her hands forward, grasping at the air in front of her, her breath shallow and uneven. Slowly, she edged to her right, where she expected Chandra to be. Her fingers brushed against the fabric, then the familiar slender hand—*this had to be Chandra.*

"Chandra! Chandra!" she called out frantically, shaking her. But Chandra remained stiff, like a statue. Smitha ran her hands over Chandra's face. It was expressionless—frozen in place, as though all life had drained from her. Her eyes were open but vacant, unblinking.

"Please, Chandra! Say something!" Smitha's voice cracked, but there was no response, no sign of recognition.

Standing inside the shrine and facing the doors, Smitha caught a glimpse of the divine creatures behind Chandra. '*It looks like they've decided to wait outside,*' she thought in frustration. Desperation clawed at her as she called out, "Help! I don't know what to do."

The feline was the first to enter the shrine, followed by the bird and then finally the hound. They brought an air of calm with them. The feline approached Chandra, its soft purring filling the silence. It gently rubbed its head against what appeared to be Chandra's legs.

Though it did nothing to wake Chandra, the cat's presence offered Smitha a small but much-needed sense of comfort. She knelt down and brushed over the cat's fur with her trembling hand, grounding herself in its warmth, if only for a moment.

The bird perched itself on what seemed like thin air. Smitha assumed it was Ayisha, as she could only see the glowing creatures through her celestial vision. Her heart raced, but the creatures' calm presence helped steady her.

Now, at her feet, the celestial hound looked up at her expectantly.

"Take me to Ayisha," she whispered, her voice laced with hope. The hound obliged, walking silently ahead, its steps measured and deliberate. Smitha followed closely behind. Her gaze was fixed on the bird, trusting that the hound was guiding her to Ayisha.

Each step toward the glowing bird felt like stepping through a veil between worlds, her uncertainty pressing down on her—but the creatures' quiet companionship kept her going.

"Ayisha! Wake up!" Smitha instructed, but Ayisha remained unresponsive.

Slap! Standing directly in front of her, Smitha slapped Ayisha as hard as she could.

"Ow! That hurt," Ayisha complained, squeezing her eyes shut in pain and pressing her hand to her stinging cheek. "What did—"

"Don't look. Keep your eyes closed," Smitha interrupted, quickly placing her hand over Ayisha's face.

"What? Why?" Ayisha asked, bewildered.

"You were out for a long time. I don't know what happened, but let me wake Chandra up first," Smitha said urgently. "Whatever you do, don't open your eyes. No matter what."

Ayisha's face twisted with fear, her voice trembling. "Don't go, I'm scared. I can't see anything... I don't have your divine vision."

Smitha stroked her cheeks and spoke softly. "It's alright, Ayisha. I'll wake Chandra up. In the meantime, put your hand on your shoulder."

She guided Ayisha's hand. "Can you feel your guide? She's perched right there. She'll take care of you."

"Okay," Ayisha whispered, her voice small and frail. She gripped her shoulder where the bird was perched.

With the hound leading the way, Smitha moved toward Chandra. The fear that had once engulfed her was now gone. It was replaced by a newfound confidence.

She tried the same tactic she had used on Ayisha, slapping Chandra's cheeks. But no matter how hard she slapped, Chandra remained unresponsive.

"Smitha, what's going on? Did Chandra wake up? I can't hear her," Ayisha called out from across the room, her voice filled with concern.

"She's not waking up," Smitha replied, frustration creeping into her tone. "I don't know what else to try. Should we drag her out of here?"

"That could be risky," Ayisha replied, thinking quickly. "Why don't you block her view with your bag and then splash water on her face? Maybe the shock will bring her back."

"That's a good idea," Smitha agreed, pulling out her water bottle. She positioned her bag in front of Chandra's face, carefully blocking her view. Once she was sure Chandra's sight was obstructed, Smitha splashed the cold water onto her face, hoping the shock would jolt her awake.

"Why did you do that? The water went into my eyes!" Chandra yelled, rubbing her face in irritation.

Smitha was relieved that she was finally alright. She quickly responded, "Don't open your eyes, just keep them closed."

"What? Why? What's going on?" Chandra asked, her confusion rising.

"I'll explain everything later. Right now, we need to get out of here. Hold my hand and walk with me, but whatever you do, don't open your eyes," Smitha instructed, her tone firm but calm.

Chandra hesitated but agreed, reaching out and grasping Smitha's hand.

Smitha guided her carefully as they moved towards Ayisha. "Ayisha, I'm right here. Can you feel my hand?"

"Yes," Ayisha responded, clutching Smitha's hand tightly.

"Good. Now, follow me slowly. Keep your eyes closed, no matter what," Smitha reminded them both, her voice steady despite the tense situation.

Smitha followed the glowing pathway out of the shrine with her spectral hound leading the way. The tension in her chest began to ease with each step as they moved further from the eerie silence within. Once they were well outside, she stopped and turned to the others.

"We're outside now," she said, her voice steady but firm. "You can open your eyes. But do it only if you're facing forward. Do *not* turn back and look at the shrine."

Chandra and Ayisha cautiously opened their eyes.

"Wow," Ayisha breathed. "That was... something else."

"That was an experience," Chandra added, a mixture of awe and lingering fear in her voice.

Smitha, relieved but still filled with curiosity, asked, "Now, can you two explain what exactly happened in there?"

Chandra and Ayisha exchanged uncertain glances. Their memories surfaced slowly, yet instead of fear, a sense of wonder began to take hold.

"When we were inside... it wasn't what I expected," Chandra began softly, her eyes reflecting the memory. "It was beautiful. The moonlight streamed through a small opening in the ceiling, right above the altar. It shone like a spotlight from above. It felt like we were standing in the presence of something ancient and sacred."

Ayisha nodded, her expression lightening as she recalled the details. "Yes, it wasn't dark at all. The moonlight fell on these three statues—headless, yes, but there was something serene about them. We were... entranced."

Chandra continued, her was voice filled with awe. "The two statues at the back were so distinct. The one on the right looked like a nomad, dressed in simple robes and holding a staff. There was something humble about it, as though it had journeyed across vast stretches of time itself."

"And the one on the left," Ayisha added, "it was seated on a platform. Adorned with jewellery, four arms, holding a conch and chakra. It looked like a Vishnu statue but different somehow. It was majestic."

Smitha's interest was piqued, and she leaned in slightly. "And the statue in front? What did it look like?"

Chandra smiled softly. "It stood tall in the centre, dressed in fine clothes, like the others, but... it felt more human. Well adorned but grounded. There was something familiar about it like it represented the connection between our world and the divine."

Ayisha sighed almost dreamily, "It didn't feel real. It felt like we were being transported to another world, a pleasant dream. I think that's why we were stunned. The beauty of it all... it was too overwhelming."

Smitha, now beginning to understand, felt a sense of relief. "I thought you both were cursed. Maybe that's why I felt like wearing the blindfold."

"Yes," Chandra agreed. "It was like the shrine was inviting us to witness something... beyond our understanding. We were too captivated to react. I don't think we'll ever fully understand what we saw," she said, her voice calm but filled with wonder.

Ayisha, ever the dreamer, smiled faintly. "It felt like we were chosen to witness something... otherworldly like we were allowed a glimpse of a hidden truth."

While being careful not to glance in the direction of the shrine, Smitha removed her blindfold. The area around them was just as Chandra and Ayisha had described. The moonlight illuminated the ground, where several heads were placed carefully on platforms lining the pathway.

She stepped closer to the ornate statue, her gaze landing on the head with an intricately designed crown. The craftsmanship was stunning, every detail precise. "Is this the head of God Vishnu?" she wondered aloud, her voice filled with reverence.

The others gathered around her, drawn to the scene. "It looks like it," Ayisha murmured, carefully scanning the heads around them, "Does that mean each of these heads belongs to a statue inside?"

Smitha nodded slowly, her mind working through the pieces. "That could be the case. Each head here must correspond to one of the statues inside the shrine."

She turned to the divine creature that had accompanied them—the glowing animal still beside her. Its serene presence felt reassuring as if it understood everything. "Is that the truth?" she asked softly, looking into its deep eyes.

The hound nodded, as if understanding her words perfectly, confirming what they had all begun to piece together.

A sense of calm settled over the group. They had uncovered one small piece of the puzzle. However, the larger mystery remained. As they stood there, bathed in the moonlight, they felt a quiet understanding pass between them and the divine presence that had guided them.

"Well, what do you want us to do?" Chandra asked, half-expecting the hound to open its mouth and speak.

Suddenly, a strong, cold wind swept through the three of them. Chandra felt herself pulled into the deep, endless abyss of the animal's eyes. She was transfixed, and in that moment, visions filled her mind. She saw the three statues inside the shrine, now with their heads intact, standing in their full, restored glory. Just as suddenly as it had begun, the vision faded, and she was back where she started, as if nothing had happened.

"Wow, did you experience that?" Smitha asked, her voice trembling with awe.

Chandra glanced at the others, and they all nodded in silent agreement. "That was the vision," Chandra said slowly, piecing it together. "We're supposed to reunite the heads with the bodies of the statues."

She turned to the hound, her eyes filled with questions. "Why us?" she asked, hoping for an answer.

But the creature remained silent.

Smitha, undeterred, stepped forward and addressed the hound directly. "Do you want us to return the heads to the statues?"

The hound gave a slow, deliberate nod as though it would only respond to Smitha.

"Can we come back and do it tomorrow—during the day? Maybe get some help?" Ayisha asked thoughtfully.

But the hound shook its head firmly as if disagreeing with her.

Chandra raised an eyebrow. "I guess it's only yes or no questions then," she said half-mockingly. To her surprise, the hound nodded in response.

Smitha glanced between them. "Should we do it tonight?" she asked cautiously.

The hound nodded again.

Chandra, now more curious, frowned. "Is it because this magic, or whatever it is, only works at night?" she asked, suspicion creeping into her voice.

Once more, the hound nodded and then gazed up at the sky. A beam of light from the moon fell upon it, illuminating the creature in an ethereal glow as though on cue.

Chandra's eyes widened as understanding dawned on her. "The moon... that's your source of power," she said, the realization hitting her.

The hound gave one final, confirming nod.

After a moment of deep thought, Smitha asked, "Does this mean you want this done before the full moon in a few days?"

The hound stared at her momentarily, then nodded, almost as if surprised by her insight.

Smitha looked at the others. "So, what do you think? This feels like a Herculean task ahead of us."

"Let's do it," Ayisha chimed in quickly.

Chandra and Smitha turned to her in surprise. "That was a quick decision," Chandra remarked.

Ayisha shrugged, a playful smile on her lips. "Well, it's not every day you get to deal with something... otherworldly. This is a once-in-a-lifetime opportunity. And who knows? We might be rewarded for our efforts in the end," she added with a mischievous grin.

Smitha scoffed. "I agree. The adventure alone might be worth it. What about you, Chandra?"

Chandra beamed. "I'm in!" After a moment, her expression shifted to concern. "But moving all three heads will take a lot of time and energy. I'm already exhausted."

Smitha nodded in agreement. "I'm tired too."

Ayisha offered a solution. "If that's the case, we can do one statue at a time. But first, let's check if the hound is okay with us pushing the rest to tomorrow."

Smitha turned to the hound, her voice hopeful. "Can we do just one statue today? We'll finish the others tomorrow—definitely before the full moon."

The hound nodded enthusiastically, its tail wagging as if relieved and thrilled that they had all agreed.

CHAPTER 9

The night air felt cooler as the trio stood under the soft glow of the moon. Their task was now clear, but its weight was beginning to sink in. Smitha glanced at the statues' heads resting solemnly on their platforms, casting long shadows on the ground. Each one seemed to hold a secret, an ancient purpose that only they could unlock. The celestial beings stood silently by their side as if waiting for them to make the first move.

Despite the enormity of what lay ahead, a quiet determination stirred within her. She felt that this night marked the beginning of something far more significant than she had ever imagined.

"What do we do now? Move the heads into the shrine and call it a day?" Ayisha asked nonchalantly, her voice breaking the silence. Her attempt to appear casual couldn't mask the undercurrent of tension lingering in the air.

Smitha let out a deep sigh, "No, it's not that simple," she said, her tone firm. "We'd have to be blindfolded, remember?"

"Oh," Ayisha muttered, the disappointment evident in her voice, her earlier bravado waning.

Chandra, still staring at the statues, furrowed her brow. "So, what's the plan?" she asked, her voice soft but steady.

"Let's not panic," Smitha said, her voice now carrying an authoritative edge that cut through the night's stillness. "First, let's try to lift the head off the platform—together, all three of us. We need to see how heavy it is before anything else. After that, we'll blindfold ourselves and go back inside the shrine. We'll feel the statues to understand where the heads need to be placed. Then, we'll carry the heads in."

Chandra carefully observed Smitha's explanation and nodded. "That sounds like a solid plan," she said, her voice filled with newfound resolve.

Smitha met the celestial hound's gaze, her expression calm and unwavering. "Please guide us when we are blindfolded," she said. The hound gave a slow, deliberate nod, its eyes gleaming with an almost knowing understanding.

Smitha then turned to the others. "Should we start with Vishnu's head? It feels auspicious to begin with a God," she suggested, her voice calm yet imbued with a subtle sense of awe.

"Yes, let's," Chandra agreed with a determined nod.

They approached the platform where Vishnu's head rested. They paused for a moment, taking in the scene before them. The head, ornate and grand, seemed even more majestic under the moon's silver gaze. It gleamed softly, its intricate carvings catching the light as if it was ready to return to its rightful place.

"Alright, time to focus on the task at hand. On three," Smitha instructed, her voice cutting through the stillness of the night. "One, two, three—go!"

Together, they carefully lifted the heavy head, each moving with deliberate care as though they were handling something fragile. The cool stone was smooth beneath their fingertips, but its weight was undeniable, pulling their muscles in different directions as they tried to keep it steady.

"Let's hold it for ten seconds," Smitha called out.

The seconds passed slowly, the stillness of the night surrounding them, punctuated only by their measured breaths. "One, two, three, four... ten," she counted softly.

"Now, let's drop it. One, two, three—go," she commanded.

With a practised motion, the three of them lowered the stone head back onto the platform, each feeling relief at its return.

Ayisha let out a soft chuckle, the tension leaving her body. "It wasn't that hard. We can definitely carry this all the way inside," she said, her voice light with surprise at how manageable it had been.

"That's true," Smitha agreed, her gaze fixed on the statue. "But what about trying it blindfolded?"

"That's a good idea, let's do that," Chandra said, her voice steady with determination. "But how do we blindfold ourselves?" she added, glancing around as if expecting a solution to appear.

Smitha pondered for a moment. "I can tear my shawl into two. I can't tear it into three, though," she said, assessing the fabric.

Chandra gave a small smile. "You can give the second piece to Ayisha. I have a shawl, but it's too small to be torn into more than one."

"Alright, that works," Smitha replied with a nod. She quickly grasped the edges of her shawl and made a small tear down the middle with a sharp tug of her teeth. The fabric gave way easily, the tear ragged but effective. She pulled it apart, dividing the cloth into two pieces.

"Thanks," Ayisha said, her fingers brushing over the soft fabric before she wrapped it tightly around her eyes. The cloth settled snugly, cutting off her sight but not her awareness of the surroundings—the soft rustling of the trees, the cool night air against her skin.

Chandra followed suit, using her own shawl to blindfold herself, taking a moment to adjust the cloth until it fit securely. She would have to rely on touch, sound, and instinct now. She was no longer able to see the statues or the surroundings clearly, but she was attuned to something deeper, something unseen.

After seeing Chandra tie her shawl, Smitha tied her own. Her supernatural vision returned, and she was confident that she could lead the other two.

"Are we ready?" Smitha asked, her voice low but filled with purpose.

"Yes," both Ayisha and Chandra answered in unison, their voices steady and confident despite the uncertainty that lingered in the air.

The three of them gathered around the Vishnu statue once again. On cue, they lifted the statue's head carefully, their hands gripping it with firm determination. The weight of it seemed more manageable now, as if the task had become familiar with each repetition.

After placing the statue back on the platform, Smitha smiled. A sense of accomplishment settled over her. "Let's try entering the Shrine," she declared, her excitement barely contained. The success of lifting the head without sight had emboldened them, and the unknown within the shrine no longer seemed as daunting.

Looking at the celestial hound, she asked, "Can you guide us?" The hound nodded once again, its presence emanating a quiet, unspoken confidence. Smitha could see the other celestial beings returning, each one drawn back to their respective companion. The feline walked in the direction of Chandra while the bird took its place near Ayisha.

Chandra could feel the feline's soft, warm presence brush against her feet, its gentle purring filling the air with an almost calming rhythm. And then, as though a veil had been lifted, she could see. The world around her shifted, like a dream taking shape from a haze of glowing lights, but clearer now—more defined. She could make out the feline beside her, its fur shimmering with an ethereal glow.

"Wow, I now have the *divine* vision!" she exclaimed, her voice filled with wonder. The world had changed as though her senses had been expanded. She had been given her access to a realm of clarity she had never known before. The intricate beauty of the Shrine, previously hidden from her sight, now unfolded in breathtaking detail.

"So do I," Ayisha chimed in, her voice filled with excitement. "It happened the moment the bird perched on me!"

"That's great. Now, all of us can see it. Shall we try entering the shrine? Let's follow the hound," Smitha said, her voice steady, with an undercurrent of eagerness.

"Let us hold our hands," Chandra added, extending her arms.

Both Smitha and Ayisha grasped Chandra's hands firmly, the connection grounding them in the present moment. With Chandra at the centre leading the way, the trio began walking towards the body of the Vishnu statue. The hound, as though it had an invisible leash on them, moved steadily in the direction of the shrine. Its steps were slow but purposeful. The three followed behind, staying close and trusting the path ahead.

"Towards the left. Vishnu is behind the first statue on the left," Chandra reminded, her voice soft but clear in the stillness of the night. She felt the reassuring pull of the hound leading them, its steady steps guiding them toward the shrine that loomed just ahead.

Smitha looked at the hound and asked, "Can you make us see the statues better?"

As though the moon itself had heard her request, the room seemed to come alive with a soft, radiant glow. A beam of light streamed down from the ceiling, casting an ethereal luminance over everything in the shrine. The statues were bathed in this new, otherworldly glow, their features now more evident than ever before.

It wasn't the regular moonlight that had illuminated the room earlier but a shimmering, almost magical light that seemed to pulse with the rhythm of the night. The wisps, whose tendrils swayed gently, had also entered the room, adding to the enchantment. Their presence cast long, graceful shadows that made the statues appear even more grand and mystical.

As the trio moved closer to the Vishnu statue, their senses heightened. They extended their hands and touched the statue to get a feel for the figures in front of them. The air around them felt charged with the energy of the ancient beings they were about to interact with.

"It's not too high. We should be able to lift the head and place it," Chandra remarked, her voice steady but laced with a trace of excitement.

"Yes, I've also gotten the hang of it. Let's get to work," Smitha said, her tone determined.

"Okay, lead the way. I'll follow you guys," Ayisha said, her voice full of trust as she stepped closer to the others.

Together, they moved out of the shrine. The soft glow of the moonlight trailed behind them as though reluctant to let them go. The air outside felt crisp and cool, carrying the scent of night-blooming flowers, while the ground beneath their feet was solid yet hummed faintly with the energy of the shrine.

They approached the platform where Vishnu's head rested, ready for the task ahead. Just as they had practised earlier, they repeated the steps with careful coordination. As the last step, they placed the Vishnu's head on top of the stone body inside the shrine. The moment they placed it onto the body, it settled perfectly—magnetically, as if the statue had been waiting for this reunion for centuries.

As they stepped back to admire their work, a soft hum filled the air, resonating through the ground beneath them. The statue glowed brighter for a moment before settling into a steady, gentle light. It seemed almost alive, as though infused with an ancient energy. The first part of their task was complete.

Smitha wiped her brow, feeling a rush of satisfaction. "One down," she said quietly, glancing at the others.

Chandra nodded, a smile tugging at her lips. "It's a start."

"Two more to go," Ayisha whispered, still holding onto a sense of awe.

With that, they turned around and walked out of the shrine.

"Should we finish the remaining tasks right away?" Ayisha asked, a hint of impatience creeping into her voice.

"No, let's not do that," Chandra said firmly. "We've got time until the full moon, and it's already 11 PM. If we push ourselves, we'll miss the last bus back."

Ayisha looked at her incredulously. "Really? We're worried about a bus right now?" Her voice was sharp with disbelief. "You do realize we're dealing with a divine task, right? Why is the bus even significant in the grand scheme of things?"

Smitha, sensing the tension, stepped in to smooth things over. "Chandra's got a point," she said calmly, her tone measured. "Let's say we do manage to finish by midnight or even one a.m. What then?"

Before Ayisha could jump in again, Smitha pressed on. Her voice was steady but firm, "You mentioned celestial protection keeping the wild animals at bay. But what happens if that protection fades the moment we're done? If the celestial beings disappear, how do we safely return to the main road? Even if we did get to the main road, are we supposed to wait in the middle of nowhere until the next bus shows up in the morning?"

Ayisha's face tightened, and her brow furrowed in frustration. She opened her mouth to argue but paused. The logic tugged at her resolve. Despite the undeniable practicality of it all, she still wasn't fully convinced.

Noticing her reluctance, Chandra softened her tone. "I get it," she said gently. "This is a once-in-a-lifetime experience, and stopping now feels like missing out. But we need to be smart about this." She paused momentarily before adding, "Just imagine this place without the willows lighting the path. We don't even have drinking water. Aren't you thirsty?"

Ayisha considered her words; the dryness in her throat became more noticeable now that Chandra had mentioned it.

"Let's head back for tonight," Chandra continued. "We can come back tomorrow with snacks, water, a good torchlight, and fully charged phones. That way, we'll be comfortable and ready for anything."

Ayisha sighed, a reluctant smile tugging at the corner of her mouth. "You're right. Even the thought of getting stuck in the forest is giving me goosebumps." She glanced around, her mind painting vivid images of the dark, silent woods. "We'll come back tomorrow," she said, shuddering.

Smitha nodded in agreement, her relief evident in her expression. "Good choice," she said with a smile.

"Come on, let's head back to our room." Chandra linked her arm with Ayisha's, playfully skipping toward the shrine's exit. Smitha followed behind, shaking her head with an amused grin.

As they made their way out, Smitha turned to the hound, who had been patiently watching them. "We'll come back tomorrow," she said. "Can you lead the way back?"

With a knowing nod, the hound trotted ahead, taking the lead on the now-familiar path through the forest. The trio followed closely behind, as the moon lit their path as they walked back towards the safety of their lodging.

CHAPTER 10

The next morning arrived. The three friends had settled back into their lodging, and the previous night's excitement was still lingering in the air. While bundled up cosily under her blankets, Smitha mumbled sleepily, "Wow, yesterday was eventful. How are you both awake? It's just 9:00 AM!" She glanced at Ayisha and Chandra, who were sitting in her room, bright-eyed.

Ayisha and Chandra shared a room at the Airbnb apartment. Their room had a large east-facing window that allowed the morning sunlight to flood in—the golden rays gently coaxing them awake. However, Smitha had opted for the darker and more secluded room, where the sun's reach was minimal, making it the perfect haven for late risers. Yet, it was becoming a habit for Chandra and Ayisha to migrate to her room in the mornings, a ritual that started long before their current adventure.

Lounging on a dull red sofa in her baggy T-shirt and shorts, Chandra sipped her coffee and grinned, "The real question is, how did you even manage to sleep after last night?" Her voice carried a playful tease, but the curiosity was genuine. She couldn't shake the vivid memories of the shrine, the statues, and the strange, magical occurrences.

Smitha gave a sleepy smile in response, still too wrapped up in her warm cocoon to formulate an answer.

"Get up!" Ayisha called out, her voice filled with energy as she sat comfortably at the foot of Smitha's bed, leaning against the wall with a wide grin. "We've got so much to talk about!"

Her excitement was infectious, and although Smitha was reluctant to leave her cosy spot, she knew Ayisha was right. The previous night's events were too incredible to ignore. Before they could return to the shrine for the next phase of their adventure, there was a lot to process.

Smitha stretched under the covers, reluctantly peeling herself away from the warmth. "Alright, alright, I'm up," she muttered, rubbing her eyes and stifling a yawn. Still cocooned in her blankets, she sat up slowly, blinking away the remnants of sleep. "Give me 10 minutes. I'll be back," she added with a sleepy smile, carefully sliding off the bed.

As she shuffled toward the bathroom, her voice floated back, "You ordered breakfast, right?" The question hung in the air, not directed at anyone in particular.

"Yes, it's already on the dining table, along with coffee," Chandra responded, glancing up from her mug.

Smitha gave a small nod, acknowledging Chandra's words as she continued her slow, groggy journey to the bathroom. The morning light filtered faintly into the room, casting a soft glow. The day's conversation lingered in the air, waiting for her return.

Soon, the three friends sat around the room, wide awake, with coffee mugs in hand and a breakfast package spread across the study table. The warm aroma of freshly brewed coffee filled the air, mixing with the faint morning sunlight streaming through the window.

"So, yesterday wasn't a dream, right?" Smitha asked, her voice filled with disbelief, as though she hadn't entirely convinced herself of the events.

Ayisha chuckled, shaking her head. "No, it wasn't. We all went through the exact same thing. So, you asking that over and over won't magically turn it into a dream," her smile widened as she took a bite of her sandwich.

Chandra nodded in agreement, "Yep, definitely real. And we've got the task ahead of us to prove it wasn't some shared hallucination." After a pause, she added, "So, what do we do today? Make a small backpack for the evening and start out late?"

"Yes!" Ayisha replied, her eyes lighting up with excitement. "We should rest as much as possible during the day. If we go a little early, we might be able to move both the statues tonight."

Smitha, who had been scrolling through her phone, suddenly looked up, her expression shifting to something more focused—her game face.

Chandra caught the shift and sighed in exasperation. "What? Don't tell me you've got an itinerary for today that you don't want to miss?"

"No, no, but listen to me," Smitha pressed, trying to convince Chandra. "Why don't we rent scooters for today? That way, we don't have to depend on the bus. There are a couple of rentals nearby that we could use."

"That's a good point," Ayisha said, warming up to the idea.

Chandra nodded, but she squinted, sensing there was more. "But that's not your entire point, is it?"

Smitha smiled, *'Chandra knows me so well'*, she thought to herself. "Okay, hear me out. Why don't we go to the park during the day, walk around, and explore a bit? We can also talk to that couple we met yesterday and see if we can visit the shrine during daylight."

Chandra furrowed her brow, deep in thought. "That is actually a good idea. It might give us more clarity on what we're dealing with. Then, let's leave as early as possible."

"What?" Ayisha groaned. "I don't want to stay out all day! Especially at the park. I'll barely have any energy for tonight."

Chandra took a deep breath and responded, her tone a mix of patience and frustration. "Yes, I know. But hear me out. It's better to go scouting while the sun's still up." She laid out the plan, "First, we rent two scooters. Then, we head to the park, do some exploration, talk to that couple, and see if we can check out the shrine during the day."

Turning to Smitha, she added, "By the way, check if you still have the key. Hopefully, it didn't vanish."

Smitha immediately got up and unzipped the small pouch of her bag. "Yes, the key's still here." She pulled out the large, ornate key to show them, then quickly put it back, relieved.

Without pausing, Chandra resumed. "After that, we can come back to our room, rest for a bit, grab snacks, get whatever else we need from the supermarket, and then head out again in the evening."

"Okay," Ayisha muttered, clearly less enthusiastic. The idea of the day stretching out with errands and planning felt more tedious than exciting.

Seeing Ayisha's disappointment, Chandra softened her tone. "Hey, I know it sounds like a lot, but it'll help make tonight easier. Plus, with the scooters, we won't be stuck waiting for buses."

Smitha took a deep breath before adding, "And a couple more things." Her voice was steady, but there was a hint of hesitation.

Chandra raised an eyebrow. "What else?"

Smitha paused for a moment before continuing. "We can't go early. We have to wait until the gates are locked and sneak in afterwards. Otherwise, the couple won't let us in. And..."

"And?" Chandra prompted, sensing something more was coming.

"And, can we maybe move the third head tomorrow, not today?" Smitha asked, her tone uncertain.

"Why?" Chandra and Ayisha said in unison, exchanging puzzled glances.

Smitha hesitated, trying to find the right words. "The dog said the full moon was important. What if something significant happens on the full moon? What if it's tied to completing the task?"

Ayisha was quick to respond. "We could just finish the task today and still visit tomorrow."

Chandra, however, seemed to ponder Smitha's words. "It's not the same," she finally said. "We can complete the task tomorrow. But I do think we need to understand the significance of the full moon better before rushing things."

Smitha's eyes lit up. "Exactly! We can do some research at the local library. And that couple! We can ask them—they'll know the local folklore and what the full moon might mean."

Chandra nodded thoughtfully. "That's a good point. It might give us more insight into what we're getting ourselves into. So, let's stick to our plan today, but only do one statue. We can leave the final piece for tomorrow."

Chandra and Smitha then turned to Ayisha, waiting for her input.

Ayisha looked between the two and sighed. "Alright, that sounds like a plan. Let's do that."

With their decision made, the three set off towards the park.

CHAPTER 11

The three friends entered the park, this time using the front entrance by the main road. Smitha's second visit was just as exciting as her first, though the atmosphere felt different in the bright mid-day sun. The vibrant colours of the park seemed even more vivid than before—flowers in full bloom, lush greenery, and the sparkling water of the fountain reflecting the sunlight. Everything seemed to pop in the daylight, creating a serene, picturesque scene.

"Wow, this place is so beautiful!" Ayisha exclaimed, her eyes wide as she took in the view.

"I told you!" Smitha replied with a smug smile, clearly pleased with Ayisha's reaction.

Although the park wasn't as crowded as it had been during the evening, a few families were still enjoying the day. Children ran around laughing, their playful energy filling the space. The scene of families spread across the green lawns and the occasional sound of a ball being kicked in the distance was comforting. It was the kind of place that made you feel at peace, the type of day that felt endless and full of possibilities.

Smitha watched a young boy chase after a butterfly, his laughter echoing through the park, and sighed in contentment. "There's something about this place, isn't there? It's just... nice to see everyone so happy and carefree."

Chandra nodded, taking in the view as she stretched her arms above her head. "Yeah, it's a good spot. Peaceful."

Ayisha, usually the one who wants to rush through everything, looked surprisingly relaxed. "I get it now," she said softly, watching a couple stroll hand in hand by the flowerbeds. "Why you love this place so much."

The three of them stood for a brief moment, soaking in the park's calmness and the warmth of the sunlight on their skin. Then, they continued their stroll towards the far side, where they hoped to come across the shrine.

"So, do you know where the shrine might be?" Chandra asked, glancing over at Smitha. "If we walk around the building towards the right, I assume we'll find it?"

"Or should we check the hilltop viewpoints first and get a better view of the surroundings?" Ayisha suggested, pointing towards the paths that led upwards.

Smitha shook her head with a small smile. "No need for the detour. You wouldn't get a good view of the shrine from up there, anyway. Let's stick to going around the park first, then we can head up."

"Alright," Ayisha agreed, though she glanced curiously toward the building leading to the hilltop before falling in line with Smitha's plan.

Suddenly, Chandra stopped in her tracks, her brow furrowing with concern. "Wait, what if we end up near the couple's house?" she asked. "The fruits are still in the scooter, and food is not allowed inside the park. We'd be empty-handed when we meet them."

Ayisha sighed. Her tone was slightly annoyed. "See? This is why I said bringing the fruit wasn't necessary in the first place."

Chandra shook her head, her expression resolute. "No, bringing something when visiting someone's home is customary. Fruits are always a safe option, especially if we're trying to apologize for showing up unannounced again. It'll help us make a better impression."

Sensing the tension in Chandra's voice, Smitha placed a reassuring hand on her shoulder. "We'll figure it out along the way," she said calmly, her tone warm and comforting.

Chandra let out a breath and nodded, feeling more at ease. "Yeah, you're right," she replied. "We'll make it work."

The trio continued along the small trail, cutting through the well-mowed lawn of the park. As they walked deeper, the trees began to grow denser, casting shadows that gave the air a cool, earthy scent. It wasn't long before they reached a tall, wire-meshed fence, halting their progress. Beyond the fence, the park continued, still well-maintained but clearly restricted from the public eye.

Ayisha glanced at the fence and sighed. "I guess this is the end."

"Looks like it," Chandra said, running her fingers along the cold metal. "We're definitely not supposed to go beyond this point."

Smitha, always quick to move on, shrugged, "Alright then. Let's head up to get a bird's-eye view of the shrine.

We can have our lunch at the canteen and then meet the couple. Sounds like a solid plan to me."

Chandra chuckled, her eyes narrowing playfully. "Why are you so obsessed with the canteen, Smitha? We're practically on an adventure, and all you can think about is food!"

Smitha flashed a grin. "Well, adventurers get hungry too, you know. Besides, park food just hits differently."

"That's fine. I'm starving too," Ayisha added, rubbing her stomach in agreement. "But I refuse to walk through that crowded children's playhouse. I can't handle near-collision with a horde of tiny humans running around. Let's take the lift directly to the terrace."

"Agreed," Smitha said with a wide smile, clearly relieved. "No more dodging toddlers for me either."

With their next steps clear, the three turned back. They walked back towards the main areas of the park. The children's laughter and the distant hum of conversations grew louder as they neared the busier section of the grounds.

***

After lunch, they retraced the pathway they had walked the previous night. In the daylight, the forest felt entirely transformed. What had been hidden in shadow now revealed itself as a lush, vibrant landscape teeming with life. The sun filtered through the dense canopy, casting dappled light on the green vines that wrapped like delicate tendrils around the sturdy brown trunks. It felt like they were wandering through an elf's enchanted garden, with the soft rustle of leaves and the occasional bird call completing the scene.

Smitha was quiet, her eyes scanning the trail as they walked. While the beauty of the forest captivated her, a small part of her was distracted. She searched for the celestial hound that had guided them the night before from the corner of her eyes. As they neared the park's back gates, her shoulders slumped a little in disappointment.

Sensing the subtle shift in Smitha's mood, Chandra gently nudged her. "What's wrong?" she asked, her voice filled with curiosity and concern.

Smitha glanced up with a polite smile, trying to brush it off. "Nothing," she replied, though the wistfulness in her tone was unmistakable. "I was just looking around to see if the hound was anywhere... but I guess not." She chuckled softly, shaking her head as if to dismiss her own hopes.

Chandra smiled back warmly. "Don't worry," she said reassuringly. "I'm sure it'll find us when we need it. It seems to have a knack for showing up just in time."

Smitha nodded, her smile a little more genuine this time. "Yeah, you're probably right."

Ayisha added light-heartedly, "I don't know about the hound, but I wouldn't mind it if we didn't have to walk this far again!"

The three shared a laugh as they continued walking, savouring each other's company and the peaceful surroundings. When they reached the cottage, they noticed that there was no one outside. Taking the lead, Smitha stepped forward and knocked on the door.

Moments later, the grey-haired lady from the previous day appeared. Her face was etched with mild confusion as she saw three unfamiliar faces. She stepped out the door, her eyes narrowing slightly in curiosity. "Yes, may I help you?" she asked politely.

Smitha smiled warmly, trying to ease the situation. "Hi, I'm Smitha," she said. Gesturing to Ayisha and Chandra, who stood a little behind her, she continued, "And these are my friends. We came here late last night, and well... we accidentally trespassed on your property." She then added with a small laugh, "We wanted to give you a proper apology now that it's daylight." She extended a bag of fruits towards the old lady.

The lady's eyes widened in recognition, and her face softened into a broad smile. "Oh! It's you girls!" she exclaimed, her voice warm and inviting. "Such nice young ladies." She waved her hands dismissively, gently pushing the bag away. "You don't need to go this far, dear," she said, her tone kind and forgiving. "There's no harm done. We don't mind at all."

"No, we insist. Since we already bought them, there's nothing else we can do with them," Chandra stepped forward this time, her tone firm but polite.

The lady chuckled softly. "Okay, okay," she said, relenting. "Sit down, sit down. Let me bring you something." She motioned towards the wooden benches outside the cottage. "Our house is a little stuffy, but the air outside is lovely."

"Oh no, we don't need anything!" Smitha protested.

"Don't be silly," the woman replied with a gentle laugh as she disappeared inside briefly, returning with a plate of snacks. "Take a seat," she insisted.

The three friends hesitated for a moment but finally settled down on the benches, grateful for the hospitality. The conversation began to flow easily, their earlier nervousness melting away in the warmth of the lady's welcoming nature.

As they talked, the woman retrieved an empty plate and began slicing the fruits the friends had brought. She placed the neatly cut pieces onto a shared plate, pushing it towards the centre for everyone to help themselves.

"So, how long are you visiting Viridona?" the lady asked, her gaze warm and welcoming.

"Not long—maybe two to three weeks," Ayisha replied with a polite smile.

The lady raised her eyebrows. "That's quite a long time for such a small island," she said, amused. "But I've noticed that more and more youngsters seem to appreciate our little hometown these days. Many of them stay longer, really taking it all in."

Chandra, always curious, chimed in, "You mentioned your family has been here for generations. Did your ancestors migrate to Viridona, or have you always been on the island?"

"Oh no, we never migrated here," the woman explained with a proud smile. "We're part of the original tribal community that has lived on this island for centuries. My husband and I were both born here, just like our parents and their parents before them." She paused, then added, "Our children, though, have moved on. Our eldest lives in Vistapur, and the youngest has settled on the mainland."

Smitha, eager to keep the conversation flowing, asked, "Don't you ever feel like moving to the city to be closer to them?"

The lady chuckled softly, shaking her head. "No, my husband and I never took to the city life. It's too busy, too crowded for our liking. We prefer it here, where the air is fresh, and the hills feel like old friends." Her eyes softened as she spoke, and a contented smile spread across her face. "We know these hills well. They've been our home forever. Our sons visit often, so we don't miss them too much."

"Oh, you must know these forests like the back of your hand then," Chandra said, leaning forward slightly as she attempted to guide the conversation toward the shrine they had encountered the previous night. "We were hoping to find some local trekking groups after arriving yesterday, but we didn't come across any."

The woman shook her head lightly, a faint smile tugging at her lips. "You won't find any trekking groups here, dear. If you're looking for those, you'd have better luck south of Vistapur, around the more popular hills."

Chandra tilted her head slightly. "Why not this area? It seemed so untouched—beautiful but quiet. Almost as though no one comes here."

The woman, though still smiling, became a little more serious as her eyes flickered toward the trees beyond them. "That's because these lands are sacred. We don't venture into this part of the forest that often."

"Sacred?" Ayisha's curiosity piqued, her eyebrows rising in surprise.

The woman nodded slowly, a thoughtful look on her face. "Let me tell you a story—one that happened a long time ago," she began, her voice taking on a solemn tone. In fact, it was over a thousand years ago. It's not something most people around here would know anymore."

Smitha, Chandra and Ayisha leaned in, eager to listen to the next part of the story.

"Our tribal chief back then... Well, he had the rare gift of speaking to the Gods. One day, he had a vision—a premonition—that the waves would bring both great good and great evil to our people." The woman paused, her eyes reflecting a faraway look as though she could still see the events in her mind. "At first, we thought it meant a storm—a terrible storm. The one that would also bring new growth to the forests afterwards. That was something we could understand."

Smitha shifted slightly, her interest growing.

"But instead, it was a ship that arrived on the shore. Strange, yes, but what followed was even stranger." The woman leaned forward, lowering her voice slightly. "The ship brought with it people who were not like us. Foreigners, with things that we had never seen before— crops, tools for farming, things that helped our chief turn this place into a proper village." She looked at them, her face filled with the weight of ancient knowledge. "The Captain of the ship said that their Gods had instructed them to bring us these gifts. But there was a condition—an exchange, you might say."

Captivated, Ayisha couldn't help but ask, "What did they want in return?"

The woman's face grew serious. "They asked for land—a small, sacred piece of this island—where they could build a shrine to their Gods. The chief agreed and promised that the shrine would never be disturbed, neither by him nor his descendants. It was a tribute to the foreigners' Gods. In return, the foreigners vowed to teach us their ways so our lands could prosper."

The old lady looked at the three friends and gestured towards them. "The shrine you asked about yesterday? It's that one," she said, nodding slowly with a knowing look in her eyes. "The very same one you saw from the hilltop." She paused, glancing between the three women. "Which one of you was asking about it?"

Before anyone could respond, she waved her hand dismissively. "It doesn't matter. Just don't go near it."

Smitha, who had been listening intently, couldn't contain her curiosity. "But why? It is a temple, right? Don't people go there to pray?"

The woman's expression softened, but the gravity of her words remained unchanged. "That is true. However, these Gods were unfamiliar to us. And you must remember the prophecy—the one that spoke of a great good and a great evil." She paused, letting the weight of her words settle in the air like a heavy fog.

"We believe that the temple embodies both great good and great evil." Her voice grew quieter as though she feared the very mention of it might summon something unseen. "But then again," she added, her smile slow and almost reluctant, "our tribe flourished after the new Gods arrived."

Chandra, who had been pondering the lady's words, raised an eyebrow. "So, this temple could be the great good, right?"

The old lady let out a small, soft laugh—barely a chuckle, more a bittersweet sigh—as though the question were a familiar one that had been asked countless times before. "Ah, yes. Many of the younger ones in the village believed that. Some even found peace there, a sense of purpose. But others..." Her voice trailed off as she seemed to recall something darker. "Others met with strange, though often small, accidents inside the temple. It's as if the temple can think. It often decides who can enter, whom it will accept, and whom it will reject."

Chandra's eyes widened. "Really?"

The old lady nodded. "Yes. It's not a place to be taken lightly. Some have tried to defy its will, only to end up with misfortune." Her tone was matter-of-fact, as though this was common knowledge.

Ayisha leaned forward, intrigued. "So, you're saying the temple... it has a mind of its own?"

The lady sighed, shaking her head. "Not in the way you think. It's more like... a force, a presence. Those who enter with good intentions may leave unharmed, but others—those with ulterior motives or who disturb the balance—it doesn't take kindly to them."

Smitha, who had been silent for a moment, exchanged a glance with Chandra and Ayisha. The air between them thickened with the weight of the old woman's words. "That sounds... interesting," she said, though her voice betrayed a trace of uncertainty.

The old woman's expression hardened slightly. "It's best not to challenge old beliefs. Some things are better left undisturbed, especially when it comes to matters like these."

The ladies continued the conversation for a little longer, exchanging pleasantries and listening to the old woman's stories about the island. Her words painted a picture of life on the island—of its people, traditions, and quiet beauty. Yet, despite the lightness of the topics discussed, the shrine remained in the back of their minds, an unspoken thought that lingered just beneath the surface.

As the conversation naturally wound down, the women stood up from the benches and began gathering their things. They had listened intently, but now it was time to move on.

"Thank you for your time and for sharing your stories with us," Smitha said, standing up and preparing to leave.

With a final nod, the old woman offered a warm smile. The ladies turned to leave, walking down the path that led away from the cottage.

On the way toward their scooters, Chandra spoke first. "That was a productive conversation."

"That's true," Smitha agreed. "We learned a lot about the temple."

"It's annoying that we couldn't actually see the temple," Ayisha said with a sigh. "It would've been nice to take a look during the day."

"Well, what can we do?" Chandra shrugged. "The lady didn't want anyone near the forest. It's not like we could sneak past her either."

"Besides, her husband was probably working somewhere in the back," Smitha added. "It would've been troublesome if we ran into him. That old man seems to take these things very seriously."

Ayisha let out another small sigh. "That's true. Let's head back to the room. I want some rest before we go on our late-night adventure."

"So, you're still in on this after that warning?" Smitha asked, raising an eyebrow.

"Of course," Ayisha replied with a playful gleam in her eye. "No one knows what the great good is. Maybe we're the chosen ones. Besides, she did say it was people with bad intentions who had trouble with the temple."

"Exactly," Chandra chimed in. "And you know how these old stories get twisted. We are definitely going tonight."

Smitha smiled, feeling a sense of excitement for the adventure ahead. "Alright then."

The three friends headed back to their room, preparing for the long evening ahead.

CHAPTER 12

The night had fully awakened, casting long shadows under the dimly lit, flickering streetlights. The three friends stood at the edge of the park, their excitement hidden behind a calm facade. They had rented two scooters for their late-night adventure, parking them a short distance from the main road to avoid drawing any unwanted attention

"Let's quickly check to see if we have everything," Smitha said, her voice tinged with a hint of nervous energy.

"What's the point? If we don't have it, we don't have it," Ayisha replied in frustration, her impatience evident.

"No, the town is just 15 minutes away. We can easily go back and buy whatever we need," Smitha countered, determined to make sure everything was in order.

Ayisha rolled her eyes but said nothing further.

Smitha shook her head, brushing off the annoyance, and turned to Chandra, who was already going through the backpacks.

"Water, snacks, pet treats, torchlights... We've got everything. Two bags—one for you, one for me," Chandra said, confirming the checklist with Smitha as she handed over one of the bags.

"Thanks. Does everyone have their blindfolds?" Smitha asked, pulling hers out from her small backpack to show the others.

"Yes, mine's in the bag," Chandra replied, patting her backpack.

"Mine's in the small pouch of your bag," Ayisha chimed in, opening Smitha's bag and showing the blindfold inside.

"Alright then, looks like we're set," Smitha said, slipping on her backpack.

"Should we head toward the gate?" Ayisha asked, her eagerness clear in her tone.

"No, not yet. Let's wait a bit longer," Chandra said calmly. "Yesterday, the old lady locked the gate after we barged onto their property. Let's give them some more time to lock up and settle in for the night."

"She already knows us. I don't think she'll stop us," Ayisha countered, impatient to get things moving.

"No, no," Smitha interjected, siding with Chandra. "She gave us a clear warning. Plus, it seems like the locals take this very seriously. It wouldn't look good if they found out we were tampering with the ancient temple."

Ayisha let out a sigh but relented. "Fine. What should we do in the meantime?"

"Why don't we take a look around this area?" Smitha suggested, trying to keep things moving.

From the clearing that served as the park's makeshift parking area, the three friends wandered onto the main road. They hadn't noticed it earlier, but the sea was much closer than they had realized. The sound of waves crashing filled the night air, and across the road, they could see the moonlit water shimmering in the distance.

"Wow, it already feels like a full moon," Ayisha remarked, gazing at the sky.

"Beautiful! Just like me!" Chandra added with a grin, playfully referencing her name, which meant moon.

Smitha chuckled. "Yes, it does look like a full moon," she replied, ignoring Chandra's self-flattery. "The street is well-lit, even with these dim streetlights," she added, her voice soft as she admired the scene.

They stood mesmerized by the sight of the moon hovering over the sea, visible from all the way across the road. The almost full moon bathed the sky in a soft glow, and its reflection shimmered on the water's surface. The moon peeked down through the gaps between the trees lining the shore, casting a silvery light that seemed to dance on the waves. The sea looked like molten silver woven into the fabric of a saree, shimmering through the shadows cast by the swaying coconut trees.

"Shall we go closer to the shore?" Smitha asked, eager to see the moon's reflection on the water, imagining it like a silver serpent swimming toward the horizon.

"Come on, let's go. But be careful, the tides are rising, and it's almost a full moon," Chandra warned.

"It would be nice to have some fish fry while the salty, cold air hits us," Ayisha mused, drifting into her own thoughts.

"Let's do that sometime," Smitha said, her sense of adventure surfacing. "We can grab a parcel tomorrow or the day after and have a night picnic. Or maybe we could ask the locals about staying overnight here."

The three walked closer to the shore, watching the sea from a safe distance, captivated by its grandeur. The waves glistened under the moonlight, and they silently prayed for the moon's grace to shine on them once more.

CHAPTER 13

Sometime later, Smitha checked her watch and stood up, brushing off the dirt. "Time to go, it's 09:30 already. I think the gate would be locked by now."

Chandra and Ayisha glanced at her and nodded, rising to join her.

The three of them made their way toward the back gate, taking the side road. The path was well-lit by the moon, so they didn't need to take out their torches. Still, their eyes darted around, expecting the guardian animals to appear at any moment. They braced themselves for the inevitable shift in perception, where the world would be transformed by spirits and wisps. But the guides were nowhere to be seen.

As they continued, Ayisha broke the silence. "What if we missed the right chance? Do you think we won't have the divine intervention tonight?"

Smitha glanced over at her with a reassuring smile. "Don't worry about it. Let's get near the gates and see what happens."

The ladies approached the gate and noticed it was closed, likely locked. As they got closer, the three celestial beings appeared, seemingly emerging from behind the gates. With each step they took, the world around them began to change. What was once familiar faded away, replaced by a magical realm lit by will-o'-wisps glowing under the moon's light.

A wave of relief washed over the group as the enchanted world settled into view.

"Well, looks like the magic has begun. Shall we go ahead?" Chandra asked, a confident smile playing on her lips.

The others nodded in agreement and followed Smitha toward the gate. She retrieved the key, unlocking it just as they had done the night before. They began their journey towards the shrine once again, with the celestial beings leading the way. This time, Smitha and Chandra focused more intently on their surroundings, trying to map out the area mentally as they moved along.

As they neared the shrine, the hilltop with the viewpoint grew more defined, though it was still difficult to see beyond the soft glow illuminating their path. Despite the limited visibility, the vague outline of the hilltop stood out against the night sky. Smitha pulled out her phone, confirming what she had expected—no mobile signal. Fortunately, she had downloaded offline maps. She showed the map to Chandra, pinpointing their location with satisfaction.

Besides the rhythmic chirping of crickets and the croaking of frogs, the journey was blissfully quiet. The tension from earlier was completely gone. Confidence replaced any lingering uncertainty as they pressed forward.

Ayisha, walking ahead, was mesmerized by the moonlit beauty surrounding them, unaware of the quiet discovery happening just behind her.

At last, they reached the entrance by the wall, their goal in sight.

"Should we wear our blindfolds now?" Ayisha asked, breaking the silence.

"Shouldn't we wait until we are closer to the statue heads?" Chandra replied.

"What if we accidentally peek into the shrine? Remember, we left the door open yesterday," Smitha pointed out, concern edging her voice.

"Good point. Let's put them on now," Chandra agreed.

The three of them took out their blindfolds and ensured they were securely in place. Just like the previous day, the world around them transformed, its mystical elements flooding their senses as the blindfolds cut off their sight.

"So, where do we start now?" Smitha asked. With hands on her hips, she was ready to dive into the task.

The hound that had been silently guiding them moved toward the statue head on their left. The three followed, feeling the head with their hands.

"It's the head of the Buddha," Smitha and Ayisha said together.

"Alright, should we repeat what we did yesterday?" Smitha asked.

"Do we need to?" Ayisha countered, eager to get the job done. "We can take the head straight into the shrine. I think we know the layout pretty well."

"I guess that makes sense," Chandra replied, pausing for a moment as she visualized the shrine. "This head belongs to the statue of the man holding the stick. He stood behind the centre statue, on the right."

"Yeah, I remember," Smitha nodded. "If we're all confident, we can move it inside directly."

"Okay, let's do it," Chandra agreed.

The three ladies took their positions, placing their hands in spots where they could get a firm, comfortable grip.

"Let's lift it once, just to get a sense of the weight, and then place it back on the platform," Smitha instructed, echoing their approach from the previous night. "On the second try, we'll carry it inside."

"On the count of three—one, two, three, go!" Smitha called out.

They put all their strength into lifting the head and successfully managed it. After holding it for a few moments, Smitha counted again. "Drop it on three. One, two, three—go!"

They gently placed the head back onto the platform.

"This was easier than the first head," Ayisha said, relieved. "Probably because it doesn't hold the weight of a crown."

"Okay, once more then," Chandra chimed in, preparing herself for the next lift.

Before they could attempt again, Smitha turned to the hound and said, "Don't forget to guide us to the right statue. We couldn't have done it without you last night."

The hound nodded in response to her.

She then turned back to the statue, ready to go. "Okay, on the count of three—one, two, three, go!"

The friends lifted the stone head together, carefully making their way towards the shrine. They cautiously stepped over the threshold, crossing the front step, and then moved toward the headless Buddha. The inside of the shrine shone brilliantly, as though the darkness outside had never existed. Light poured in from the small opening in the centre of the ceiling. The floating wisps illuminated the space, making it feel almost as bright as day. Every surface seemed to glow, casting a surreal beauty over the scene.

As they neared the statue, a sense of regret crept in—they hadn't considered the height of this statue before bringing the head inside. The Buddha statue loomed taller than they had anticipated, and they realized with dismay that the three of them wouldn't be able to lift the head high enough to place it properly.

"Should we place it on the floor and figure it out from there?" Chandra asked, glancing between her friends. Almost as if in response, they heard a gentle *"Woof!"*

Perplexed, Smitha turned to the hound and asked, "Should we?" The hound shook its head in disagreement.

Smitha sighed and glanced back at the others. "I guess that's a no. It seems that we can't place it anywhere but where it belongs."

Behind her, the hound stood firm, nodding its head again.

Noticing the gesture, Chandra smiled. Her gaze shifted back to the towering statue as she mulled over their dilemma. Scanning the room, her eyes landed on something—a pillar with a carving near its base that could work as a step.

"There's a pillar right next to the statue," Chandra pointed out. "At the base, there's a carving that we can use as a step. One of us can climb up, pull the head into place, and guide it while the others hold it steady."

"So..." Smitha began.

"I'll climb the pillar and guide the process," Chandra volunteered confidently.

"Okay, but be careful," Ayisha cautioned, her voice filled with concern.

Chandra carefully backed up until her foot touched the stone pillar. She felt around with her foot, trying to find the grooves in the carving. "I think I've got it," she said. "Can you two take one step toward the statue?"

As instructed, Smitha and Ayisha stepped forward.

"Can you bear the full weight of the head until I find my step?" Chandra asked.

"That would be difficult; we'd have to switch positions," Smitha replied.

"Okay, I'll continue to hold on, but you'll be carrying most of the weight," Chandra clarified.

"That should work, let's give it a try," Ayisha said, ready to adjust.

With Smitha and Ayisha steadying the head, Chandra carefully balanced herself on the pillar's step. Once she found stable footing, she guided them closer, aligning the head with the statue. Together, they moved with precision, placing the head right where it belonged.

The instant the head was placed, a brilliant flash of light radiated from the statue. It illuminated the shrine for a brief, breathtaking moment before fading to a gentle, steady glow. The three friends could see the statue in its full splendour. The folds of Buddha's robes draped the figure with fluid grace, expertly carved to capture the soft ripples of fabric.

They stepped back to take in the sight of the entire shrine through their blindfolds. On either side of the central figure, the two statues glowed softly from within. The front and centre statue, though beautifully reflecting the surrounding light, remained unfinished.

"Wow, that's beautiful!" Ayisha exclaimed, with her voice full of wonder.

"Yes, it really is," Smitha agreed, equally mesmerized by the serene glow of the shrine.

"The centre statue stands tall, like a six-foot man. Do you think we'd be able to lift the head and place it on top?" Chandra asked, realizing that today's success was more a stroke of luck than anything else.

Catching onto Chandra's concern, Smitha responded thoughtfully, "Why don't we take a closer look at the statue and see if there's any kind of support we can use to climb up?" She began walking towards the centre statue.

The others followed, carefully inspecting the area. They ran their hands along the statue, feeling for anything that might assist them.

"I don't think there's anything we can use here," Ayisha said after a thorough check, a hint of frustration in her voice.

"Alright," Smitha said, stepping back. "Let us not break our heads now. Let's come back tomorrow and figure out a better way to handle this. I'm sure we'll come up with something."

"That sounds right," Chandra agreed, feeling more at ease with the plan.

Once everyone agreed, they stepped out of the shrine. Just as they approached the arched entryway in the wall, a sudden cold gust of wind brushed across their faces.

Smitha instinctively turned in the direction of the wind, an eerie sensation creeping over her, as if unseen eyes were watching. Though the blindfold covered her sight, a growing sense of dread made her quicken her pace toward the gate. Not wanting to alarm the others, she tried to keep her voice steady. "Shall we pick up the pace? I can't wait to take off this blindfold—my eyes are itching."

"Okay, let's run!" Chandra said in a playful tone, grabbing their hands and breaking into a jog toward the gap in the wall, catching the others by surprise.

Once they reached the archway, everyone removed their blindfolds with a collective sigh of relief.

Smitha instinctively looked toward the source of the cold wind—it came from her right, within the outer walls of the shrine. Her heart raced, but she didn't dare to glance too far inside. Instead, she kept her gaze fixed to her right, hoping to catch something—anything—but there was nothing beyond the glow of the spectral creatures that illuminated the area. It struck her then: these lights weren't just guiding them—they were acting like a boundary, a line not to be crossed at this hour.

After a long, steady look, she turned back to the path, ready to move on. That's when her eyes met Chandra's. Chandra was staring past her, also searching for something beyond the visible, an unspoken understanding passing between them. They nodded at each other, a silent acknowledgement that they had both sensed something—something unfriendly lurking in the shadows.

Before Smitha could start walking again, her eyes were drawn to the spectral creatures—the avian perched on Ayisha's shoulder, the feline by Chandra's side, and the hound loyally behind her. It dawned on her that these beings always stood on the outer edge, as though protecting them from what lay beyond. Replaying the events in her mind, she realized the only time this formation had broken was when the hound had guided her into the shrine earlier.

Smitha's mind drifted further back in the night as they were walking towards the shrine. She recalled Ayisha skipping ahead, carefree and joyful, as the bird circled above her. At the time, she had found it amusing, thinking the bird was merely following Ayisha's playful energy. But now, standing there with the cold wind brushing past her, Smitha realized the truth. The bird wasn't flying for fun—it had been on the lookout, scanning their surroundings for something unseen, something it felt they needed protection from.

"C'mon, let's move fast," Chandra whispered, her voice tense but composed as she addressed Ayisha.

"Why?" Ayisha asked, her normal voice echoing off the hills.

"Keep your voice down," Chandra replied in a casual tone, masking her concern. "You'll wake the couple. Plus, I'm starving, and I don't want to eat the snacks here. Some wild animal might show up."

"Okay, okay, let's go," Ayisha agreed, still unaware of the deeper tension.

The subtle shift in Chandra and Smitha's demeanour didn't escape Ayisha entirely, but she brushed it off as their usual overcautious behaviour. She followed their lead, walking quicker now.

Smitha cast one last glance at the spectral creatures before quickening her pace. They were maintaining their positions around the trio. Her thoughts lingered on their unseen guardianship as they made their way toward safety.

The three ladies quickened their pace, nearly breaking into a run as they approached the gate. Once there, Smitha hastily secured the lock, her hands trembling slightly with urgency. It felt as though the very air around them urged them to leave. The moment the lock clicked into place, the guardians disappeared, fading into the night as if they had never existed.

Smitha and Chandra exchanged glances, their surprise mirrored in each other's eyes. The guardians had walked them much further the previous night. Something was different today, something unsettling. Without needing to say a word, the three huddled close, walking quickly in the direction of their scooters. Ayisha, sensing the unease radiating from her friends, matched their hurried pace without question.

Once they had put a little distance between themselves and the gate, Smitha pulled out her torchlight, flicking it on to illuminate the path ahead. Her heart pounded in her chest as she scanned the road ahead and, almost instinctively, pointed the light toward the forest, hoping to spot any movement in the darkness.

But before the beam could reveal anything, Chandra rushed over, placing a firm hand over the torch and shaking her head. Chandra didn't want Smitha to draw attention to whatever it was that lay hidden in the forest. Understanding the unspoken warning, Smitha redirected the light back onto the road.

They quickened their steps, the eerie silence only broken by the soft crunch of gravel beneath their feet, until they finally reached the safety of their scooters.

A wave of relief washed over Smitha as they reached their parked scooters. She exhaled deeply as though she'd been holding her breath the entire time. Without a word, they climbed onto their vehicles, started the engines, and rode off towards the town. The quiet hum of the scooters was the only sound in the still night. The tension still lingered in the air.

None of them spoke as they made their way back to their lodgings, each lost in their own thoughts, processing the unsettling events of the evening. The familiar sight of the town's lights in the distance provided a small comfort. But even as they rode, a sense of unease seemed to follow them like a shadow that refused to be shaken.

CHAPTER 14

Back in the room, Ayisha's curiosity finally got the better of her. "What was that?" she asked, breaking the silence that had stretched since their return.

After they arrived at the apartment they had rented, Smitha and Chandra had gone straight to shower without exchanging a word, both too lost in their own thoughts. The tension was palpable, but Ayisha chose not to press them right away. She figured it was best to let things settle.

Now, with everyone settled down—Smitha tucked into her blankets with her phone, Ayisha sitting at the foot of the bed, and Chandra on the sofa—she decided it was time to ask.

"When did you two end up fighting? You were both with me the whole time," Ayisha said, her voice light but with a hint of concern.

Smitha, her eyes still on her phone, looked up, surprised. "We didn't fight!" she responded.

Ayisha frowned. "Then why haven't either of you said a word since we returned? It feels like you're avoiding each other or something."

Chandra, her gaze distant, finally spoke up. "No, it's not that," she said quietly. "Something happened. I think neither of us wanted to say it out loud because... well, once we do, it becomes real." She sighed, glancing at Smitha, who nodded in agreement.

Ayisha's confusion deepened. "What do you mean? What happened?"

Chandra let out a deep sigh. "On the way back, we both sensed something... off. Like we were being watched by something or someone. The celestial beings were trying to protect us—they were always on guard. I think the divine lights also shielded us. But we were worried that there was something *to* be protected from."

Smitha added softly, "I felt it too. That cold gust of air... and the feeling of eyes on us. And the celestial beings left us earlier than usual." She shuddered, pulling the blanket tighter around herself as if seeking warmth from the unsettling memory.

Ayisha frowned, falling into deep thought. After a moment, she turned to Chandra. "Is that why you held my hand and pushed me to walk faster? You both gave weird excuses."

"Yes, that was the reason," Chandra admitted.

Ayisha raised an eyebrow, incredulous. "Of course something was looking at us. It's a forest—what do you expect?" she said. "It could've been a wild pig or something."

Smitha shook her head, her voice firm. "No, it felt different. I felt like... it could've been a person."

Ayisha crossed her arms, still sceptical. "A person? In the middle of the night? That doesn't make any sense." She paused, considering Smitha's words more carefully. "Actually... it's possible. You heard that lady earlier; she said this place belonged to the tribals. If any kids from the village wandered off, they'd definitely be drawn to a strange, fully lit pathway, wouldn't they?" Her frustration was growing as she tried to rationalize the situation. "And the animals left because they probably felt there was no danger, not because something was wrong."

Smitha nodded slowly, though her expression remained uneasy. "That makes logical sense, but... I still can't shake off this feeling."

Ayisha sighed, her tone firm. "Look, I get it—being out there so late is scary. Even the smallest rustle can make us jump. But this is what we're going to do." She glanced between her friends, her voice taking on a matter-of-fact tone. "We'll stick to our original plan and not let these fears control us. Tomorrow, we'll go to the library and research the area to see if there are any myths or wildlife we should be aware of. Then, we'll head back and explore the shrine in the daytime before our nightly adventure."

Smitha mumbled, "Okay," trying to avoid Ayisha's eyes.

Chandra, sensing Ayisha's growing impatience, quickly agreed. "Yes, okay." She gave a small, sheepish smile as Ayisha shot her an annoyed look.

"Alright, let's go to sleep everyone. Also, tomorrow, let's buy a small plastic stool—it'll help us with the head," Ayisha suggested, her practical tone returning.

With nothing else to discuss, she made her way towards her room while gesturing for Chandra to follow. The two disappeared into the room, leaving Smitha behind, still wrapped in her blanket, deep in thought.

Smitha sighed softly, turning off her phone and placing it on the nightstand. The silence of the apartment felt unusual, but she tried to shake off the lingering unease. "It'll be better tomorrow," she whispered to herself. She pulled the blanket closer as she settled into bed, hoping for some much-needed rest.

CHAPTER 15

The three friends arrived at the library early in the morning, eager to uncover more about the local lore and mysteries surrounding the shrine. Smitha and Chandra gravitated toward the local history section, pouring over various books and documents. Their initial enthusiasm quickly waned since most texts detailed only the island's colonisation, with scant mention of anything predating that period. Frustration crept in as the shrine and its significance remained shrouded in mystery.

Meanwhile, Ayisha wandered into the flora and fauna section. Though her primary interest was the island's unique wildlife, she kept an eye out for anything that might explain the strange occurrences they had witnessed. Her curiosity was piqued by the potential link between the natural world and the inexplicable events surrounding the shrine.

After hours of consulting several sources, each of them managed to gather small pieces of relevant information—though none provided a full picture. Still, with time pressing on and a sense of urgency growing, they decided to leave the library and head directly to the park to review their findings. Settling under the shade of a sprawling bougainvillaea tree, the vibrant pink blossoms fluttering in the light breeze, the trio prepared to piece together the puzzle and discuss what they had uncovered.

"So, what did you find out?" Smitha asked.

"Let me go first," said Ayisha, sitting up a bit straighter. "I found out about a few animals we might run into. There are some deer species, but they tend to run off at the sight of humans. Then there are wild pigs, and they have a reputation for being bad-tempered, so we should avoid them. Civets too— they are small, rodent-like creatures. And as for birds, we've got eagles, some sea birds, and other smaller varieties. Oh, and a variety of snakes, though nothing particularly dangerous according to the guidebooks."

Smitha nodded thoughtfully before adding her findings. "I didn't get much from the history books, either. There's barely any record of life before colonisation, except that it was a pretty tribal existence, mostly revolving around fishing and farming. But here's the strange part—there is no mention of any stone structures or significant architecture before that period. It's as if the shrine we found doesn't even exist in the historical record."

"That makes sense," Chandra agreed. "The record-keeping started recently, so historians didn't begin exploring this island until much later. There are no records kept by the natives from before that time."

She paused for a moment before diving into her own findings. "I went through some of the old folklore, and there was something familiar. Do you remember the story the lady mentioned? It's the same one, but there's one major difference." Chandra leaned forward, her voice quieter as if sharing a secret. "Apparently, there were two prophecies that the village chief received— centuries apart. The first prophecy led to foreigners entering the village, and with them came the statues. The second prophecy, much later, seems to have prompted the construction of the shrine."

She glanced at Smitha and Ayisha, gauging their reactions. "All of this happened over a thousand years ago, but I couldn't get a precise timeline. The lores are vague about the actual dates. What's more intriguing is that the temple is believed to house a God brought over from a foreign land. According to the stories, this God is said to be very strict—extremely generous to the good, but equally harsh with the slightest wrongdoing."

Chandra continued, her voice lowering as she recounted the tales. "There are a lot of small stories that talk about how those who followed the god's rules were rewarded, but even minor misdeeds were punished severely. That's why the locals avoid the temple. They're afraid of how powerful this god is, and they believe even a small misstep could bring trouble."

Absorbing the new information, Smitha chimed in, "It does make you wonder who these foreigners were. They could've come from the mainland. We know ships passed through this area along the trade routes, but they hardly ever stopped here. They thought it was an abandoned island. Still, no records mention ships specifically chartered to come here."

"If the actual event happened such a long time ago, it could explain why the stories have so many variations," Smitha mused. "I mean, they've probably changed a lot, being passed down by word of mouth over the centuries. Did either of you find anything about why the head and the body of the statue are separate? I couldn't find any mention of it."

"No, I didn't come across anything either," Chandra admitted, frowning.

The more they uncovered, the more questions seemed to emerge. *Why were these statues brought to the island? Who was this god, feared and revered for so long? And what happened that led to the statues being disfigured?*

"Argh, having so many unanswered questions is frustrating!" Chandra burst out, throwing her hands up.

"That's alright," Ayisha said in her usual calm tone. "Look at what we've already found. And hey, the gods are supposed to protect us, right? That's comforting." She smiled, trying to lighten the mood. "Let's take a break. I'm starving. Let's go grab some food, then we can head into the forest."

Everyone smiled in agreement, the tension lifting slightly. They might not have all the answers yet, but they had uncovered more than they had expected. And with a plan in place, there was still hope for more discoveries ahead. Together, they began walking toward the canteen, eager for some food before their next exploration.

***

After their short break, the three friends made their way towards the park's back gate. As they approached the open gate, Smitha paused. Her eyes narrowed as she thought through the next step.

"Can you two wait here for a moment? I'll go ahead and check if the cottage doors are closed," she whispered, glancing at Chandra and Ayisha.

The others nodded in agreement. It seemed like a good idea to scout ahead without drawing too much attention.

Smitha moved cautiously, her steps light and deliberate, as though she were trying to blend into the very shadows of the path. She tiptoed forward, every muscle tense, ears straining for any noise that could give her away. As she neared the gate, she peeked beyond the stone walls, her breath catching in her throat for a moment.

The old cottage came into view, its weathered wooden door shut tight and the windows closed. No lights, no movement. It looked like no one had been around for some time. She scanned the surroundings again, ensuring there wasn't anyone nearby, before turning back to her friends. With a quick wave, she signalled to Chandra and Ayisha to follow. The coast was clear.

They crossed the cottage, doing their best to move quietly, not wanting to risk catching the attention of the lady who lived there. Once past it, they took the familiar path they had walked the previous two nights. Yet, in the daylight, everything seemed different. The narrow path they had tread in the dark now appeared as a simple, worn patch of land, eroded by years of foot traffic. The thorns and brambles that had gone unnoticed during the nights seemed to snag at their clothes and skin as if reminding them of the harshness of the forest in daylight.

Before long, they reached a clearing where the path ran parallel to the stone wall leading towards the shrine's entrance. With the daylight illuminating their surroundings, the friends could now see the hilltop clearly. From their vantage point, several paths sprawled across the forest, merging into the shrine's grounds. Some of these trails even led towards the hilltop, winding through the dense trees like veins. It was a detail completely hidden from them under the cover of night.

The shrine, which had loomed large and mysterious in the darkness, now seemed much smaller in the brightness of day. The grey stones that made up its walls were smooth, devoid of the intricate carvings or embellishments they had half-expected. It was plain, humble even, and much less imposing than it had felt during their nighttime visits.

As they neared the entrance arch, Smitha's eyes were drawn to the two statues of Yakshas that flanked the gate. These weren't like the usual depictions she'd seen before—broad-shouldered and slim-waisted guardians of mythology. Instead, these statues looked more lifelike, resembling real people. They stood tall and strong, though time and weather had not been kind to them. The faces were nearly eroded away, and both statues were missing one of their arms, adding a sense of fragility to what once must have been proud, fierce protectors of the shrine.

Smitha couldn't help but pause and study them for a moment. These statues, worn as they were, carried an air of dignity despite their condition as if they had silently witnessed countless events unfold over centuries.

As they crossed the statues of the strong warriors and entered the area enclosed by the walls, the three friends were surprised to find two men standing inside.

One was the grey-haired man from before whom they had encountered at the cottage. The other was a younger man who looked almost like a mirror image of the older man, as though a younger version of him had somehow travelled through time. The resemblance between the two was unmistakable—they were clearly father and son. Both men looked at the ladies with surprise, the sudden appearance of visitors catching them off guard.

Smitha, always the one to ease tension, broke the silence with a friendly greeting. "Hi! How are you?" she said with a polite smile. "Do you remember us? We accidentally came to your cottage late that night. We also stopped by yesterday to apologise," she added, hoping the old man didn't hold any grudges over their earlier intrusion.

The old man responded with a gentle smile. "Yes, I remember. It was very kind of you to visit. My wife was quite happy to have some company." His warm tone put the group at ease. "But tell me, what brings you here today?"

Chandra chimed in, taking over from Smitha. "Well, your wife told us such a beautiful and magical story about this shrine yesterday. We couldn't stop thinking about it. It's not every day you hear of something so ancient and mysterious, so we just had to come and see it for ourselves," she explained.

The old man nodded thoughtfully but then interrupted, "Why are you standing all the way over there?" he asked, noting the distance the ladies kept from the shrine's grounds.

Smitha quickly answered, "Oh, we're still wearing our shoes. We didn't want to disrespect the place by walking in with them."

The old man waved away their concern with a smile. "That's alright. I'm used to walking barefoot here, but this place can be too dangerous without proper shoes. Go ahead, walk in."

Relieved, the three friends stepped further inside. Ayisha, who had been quietly observing from behind, relaxed a little. She was content to let Smitha and Chandra handle the conversation for now.

As they walked in, the old man proudly gestured toward the younger man beside him. "This is my son," he introduced, "He's here visiting us for the weekend."

The younger man smiled at them. His expression was friendly yet filled with curiosity. There was a certain warmth in his demeanour, making the trio feel more at ease.

"Nice to meet you," Smitha said, offering a smile. "Are you the one who lives in Vistapur? Your mom told us quite a lot about you," she added, trying to keep the conversation light and friendly.

"Oh! Nice meeting you too," the young man responded, a faint touch of pride crossing his face. He seemed pleased that his mother had spoken of him to these visitors. It was a subtle but genuine reaction, the kind that shows in a son proud of his roots.

"This is an old temple of ours," the old man said, seamlessly continuing the conversation. His voice, although calm, carried a trace of sadness. "I don't know why, but sometime ago, we stopped worshipping this temple." He paused, the weight of his words settling into the air. "But our family has been the caretakers of this place for generations. We couldn't just give up on the tradition, even when everyone else did." He let out a quiet sigh, the burden of this history clearly resting on his shoulders.

Smitha, Chandra, and Ayisha exchanged glances, sensing the deep connection the old man had to this place. Despite the temple's abandonment, the family had remained faithful to their duty. It felt as though they were witnessing not just a story but a living link to the past, an old thread of tradition that had somehow endured the passage of time.

"It looks like the son of mine doesn't want to continue with the tradition and is just coming up with excuses," stated he old man with frustration clear in his voice.

"But, Dad! I know what I saw," the young man blurted out, breaking the otherwise calm conversation. His tone was pleading, desperate for someone to believe him.

"Please, Dakshan! I'm not going to hear your excuses anymore," the old man shot back, his patience clearly wearing thin. "How many times have I told you not to go into the forest when you've been drinking? And never, *never* go near *any* temple when you're inebriated—especially *this* temple," he added, his voice growing stern.

The young man, Dakshan, was insistent. "How else would you explain this? The heads were attached to the body. I'm telling you! I saw the heads attach themselves to the bodies in the middle of the night!" His voice wavered between fear and conviction, a grown man speaking like a child who'd just seen a ghost.

The old man, however, wasn't having it. "Did you see the heads fly around, open the shrine door, and place themselves on the statues?" he asked, his voice dripping with sarcasm.

"No, but I *heard* the door open and close," Dakshan shot back, frustration seeping into his voice. "I heard something moving around. When I climbed a tree to get a better look, there was no one there. It was pitch dark, but I know what I heard."

The old man let out a long, disappointed sigh. His face softened, but the exhaustion in his eyes was unmistakable. "I was unwell for a few weeks and told you to take care of the shrine. You were negligent, Dakshan. You didn't do it. You didn't even bother coming near this place. I'm assuming some tourists or trekkers tried to move the statues and fit the heads long before, and you missed it. And now you're putting it on supernatural beings and flying stones," he said, shaking his head in disbelief.

The three friends, who had been standing quietly to the side, didn't dare to interrupt this intense conversation between father and son. But as they listened, things began to click into place in their minds. Smitha, Chandra, and Ayisha exchanged glances, each processing the new information.

They realized something—when Dakshan had climbed the tree and looked into the shrine, he hadn't seen them or the celestial beings that had been guarding them. It was becoming clear that the divine lights and creatures weren't just there as decoration or coincidence. They were actively protecting the group, shielding them from prying eyes and whatever unseen dangers lurked in the forest.

The young man opened his mouth to protest again, but the father cut him off with finality. "No more buts, Dakshan. You're going to come with me every week to take care of this temple until you learn how it's done properly," the old man said sternly, his voice firm but not unkind. Then, turning to the ladies, he softened his tone. "Don't worry too much about all this," he assured them, trying to downplay the situation.

"So, this temple has three gods," he explained, gesturing toward the headless statues. "Their heads are separated from their bodies, as you can see. Only one head is placed on the outer platform. It seems that someone had tried to put the other heads back on the bodies—and they succeeded. It is unusual but not a miracle."

"But why couldn't you do it before?" Smitha asked, her curiosity piqued.

The old man sighed, shaking his head slightly. "It's not that we didn't try. We did. But the heads were too heavy to move. At some point, we just gave up," he admitted. "Perhaps the weight wasn't as heavy as our ancestors made it out to be."

Chandra, intrigued, pointed toward the last remaining head, the one still resting on the platform. The face was that of a man with a moustache, wearing a simple crown. "Are you going to try to put the last head back?" she asked, her gaze lingering on the lifelike features of the stone.

The old man glanced at the head, then shook his head with a sigh of resignation. "No," he said firmly, though there was a note of weariness in his tone. "If I were to do it, I'd need to wait for an auspicious date. This isn't something to take lightly or rush. For now, I'm just here to clean up the shrine," he added, gesturing toward a straw broom leaning against the far wall.

Chandra, sensing the conversation drawing to a close, nodded respectfully. "Oh okay, we'll let you get back to your work. Could we, by any chance, take a look inside the shrine? The one with the statues of the gods?" she asked, trying to keep her tone casual but unable to hide her curiosity.

The old man shook his head. "No, the doors are closed. We don't open them except on the day of Chitra Pournami. And that's still far away," he said, his voice carrying an air of finality.

Smitha's brows furrowed as she instinctively glanced toward the shrine. The door was indeed closed, its sturdy wooden frame looking almost forbidding in the daylight. A wave of confusion swept over her as she vividly recalled that the door had been open during their nighttime visits—ever since she had unlocked it two nights ago. *Had it been an illusion? Or perhaps... something else entirely?*

Ayisha, who had been quietly observing the exchange, noticed Smitha's puzzling expression. She decided it was time to wrap things up. "Oh, then we'll get going," she said, her voice polite but with a hint of urgency. "It was nice meeting you."

The old man smiled kindly. "Likewise. Take care on your way back," he said, turning his attention back to his broom as though the encounter had been just another passing moment in his day.

With that, the three friends took their leave. They walked out of the shrine with their voices low. As they left the temple grounds, excitement bubbled beneath their hushed tones.

"They couldn't see it, could they?" Ayisha whispered. Her eyes were wide with wonder. "The lights, the will-o'-wisps... they were only visible to us."

Chandra and Smitha exchanged glances, nodding in agreement. "It's starting to make sense," Smitha murmured. "The lights, the way we felt protected... it wasn't just a coincidence."

"And the entire thing was invisible to them," Smitha added, her voice brimming with excitement. "This means no outsider could see us. Wow! That is definitely something to think about."

"The gods are powerful," Ayisha said softly, almost in awe. "They must be watching over us, guiding us through this."

The three friends were buzzing with the thrill of the discovery. There was something more to this ancient shrine, something magical that they had been chosen to witness. Still filled with excitement and curiosity, they decided to head back to their room for a brief rest.

CHAPTER 16

Night had fallen, and the full moon rose high in the sky, casting a silvery glow across the island. Smitha, Chandra, and Ayisha stood at the entrance of the familiar road leading to the back gate of the shrine. The moonlight illuminated their path, creating long shadows of trees and bushes around them. Smitha and Chandra walked ahead, their backpacks shifting with each step, the contents rustling softly inside. Behind them, Ayisha followed, carrying two small plastic stools—tools they hoped would prove useful for the important task ahead.

"I'm so excited for tonight!" Ayisha's voice bubbled with anticipation. "Do you think we'll get to see a God? Maybe we'll even be rewarded for what we're doing. A boon, perhaps?"

Smitha smiled at Ayisha's enthusiasm. "I think we just might."

Chandra shot her a look, eyes narrowing. "Don't encourage her! You know how she is when it comes to these things." She then lowered her voice to a cautious whisper. "Also, let's not talk about this right now. Remember, we were told that the God punishes even the slightest ill intent. We need to be careful with our words, especially tonight."

Ayisha's grin faded a bit, replaced by a more serious expression. "You're right. I'll keep my thoughts to myself," she said, casting a quick glance in the direction of the shrine, her earlier excitement tempered by a newfound reverence.

The moment they spotted the gate in the far distance, something magical happened, just as it had the previous night. The celestial beings—the hound, the feline, and the bird—appeared again, materializing out of the moonlit shadows. But tonight, their energy was different. The creatures no longer carried the quiet, sombre demeanour they had shown before. Instead, they radiated a playful energy. Their movements were light and free, as if sharing in the ladies' growing excitement.

Smitha noticed the shift immediately. "They're more lively tonight," she whispered to Chandra. "Like they're happy to see us."

Chandra nodded in agreement, her cautious mood from earlier lifting slightly as the animals bounded around them. The celestial beings seemed almost joyful, as if they too were anticipating something special. For the first time in days, the girls felt a sense of companionship with these mysterious creatures, as though they were no longer just being watched but being welcomed.

The road ahead, bathed in soft moonlight, felt less daunting now. The divine lights flickered gently as if subtly guiding their way forward. Unlike previous nights, there was a palpable sense that tonight would be different. The mystery surrounding the shrine lingered in their thoughts, not as an overwhelming weight but as a quiet push that stirred their anticipation. Their task awaited, and with it came the hope of uncovering more secrets—perhaps even a glimpse of the Gods themselves.

Eventually, they reached the park gate. Smitha retrieved the key from her bag, its faint blue light casting delicate shadows over her fingers. She inserted it into the lock and twisted it, and with a soft *click*, the gate creaked open. But something unexpected happened—before Smitha could pull the key out, it dissolved into thin air, vanishing completely. Her eyes widened in surprise and excitement. "Today is the day!" she whispered with barely contained joy, turning to the others.

Chandra and Ayisha exchanged a knowing smile, their hearts pounded with anticipation. They kept their voices hushed, wary of disturbing anyone near the cottage as they continued their journey. The celestial hound trotted ahead, its tail swishing like a beacon guiding them forward.

Now that they had seen the path in the daylight, everything seemed different. Landmarks they hadn't noticed in the dark now stood out clearly: the worn-out patches of grass, the oddly twisted tree branches, and the subtle stone markers leading them towards the shrine. Yet, despite these new discoveries, the will-o'-wisps lit up the path so brightly that it almost felt like daytime. Their soft, ethereal glow bathed the area in a magical light, creating a surreal atmosphere around them.

The three friends moved silently, reverence settling over them as they neared the shrine. The stone wall loomed ahead as they approached the familiar gap that served as the entrance.

Before entering, the three of them blindfolded themselves, just as they had done on the previous nights. They knew the Gods might not appreciate prying eyes at this delicate moment. Their fingers brushed over the smooth stones at the archway as they crossed the threshold. The vision of the celestial world lingered in their minds while their other senses sharpened. Unlike their previous visits, the three ladies directly ventured deeper into the inner part of the shrine without approaching the last remaining stone head resting on the platform.

The air inside the shrine was cool and still. Their faint footsteps echoed softly off the walls with every movement. Right at the entrance, the three of them stood in awe as the will-o'-wisps illuminated every inch of the shrine. They felt almost surreal as if they had stepped into another world. The statues at the back shone brilliantly, their surfaces reflecting the ghostly light with a dazzling intensity, like stars against the deep night sky. Smitha couldn't help but think it was because of the full moon's influence, the brightness within seemed far more than what they had seen on the previous days.

They walked quietly toward the central statue, the only one without a head. With the light enhancing every detail, they could see the figure much more vividly. The tall, ornate man carved in stone stood imposing, his broad shoulders and narrow waist giving him an air of strength. His sword, gripped firmly in one hand, looked ready for battle. Smitha tilted her head, examining it closely.

"This looks like a man, not a God," she murmured, her voice tinged with curiosity.

Ayisha, frowning slightly, asked, "Why do you say that?"

Smitha gestured towards the figure. "There aren't any morphed features like multiple arms, eyes, or heads that you usually see in depictions of Gods. The posture too—it's like a human holding the sword, not an idealized or divine form. It feels more... grounded."

Chandra, always open to different interpretations, offered another perspective. "Maybe he's a human-like God. Not all divine beings look otherworldly."

"That's possible too," Smitha conceded, still intrigued by the figure's distinct lack of mythological embellishments. She stepped closer to the statue, trying to come up with a practical plan for placing the head back. "Alright, should we place the stools on either side of the statue? As close as we can, to help lift the head?"

Ayisha nodded, assessing the distance and angles. "Yes, that should work. If this head is like the others, we'll only need two of us to lift it, and the third person can help guide it into place."

Chandra agreed, her voice firm but quiet. "We'll have to be careful, but we can do this."

With a sense of purpose, Ayisha placed the stools in position, adjusting them slightly to ensure they were balanced. The three of them then exited the shrine and walked towards the platform where the final head lay waiting.

As they approached the platform, the celestial beings stood by, watching them intently but with an air of quiet reassurance. The time had come to complete their mission

Ayisha and Smitha worked in unison to lift the head, their hands steady but filled with the weight of their task. Chandra kept close, ready to lend support if they wavered. With careful steps and the head held carefully between them, they approached the shrine. As they climbed the stools and placed the head atop the statue, a sudden, overwhelming light exploded around them. The moment the head was positioned, the shrine seemed to come alive, glowing with an intensity that nearly blinded them.

The light radiated from the statues, filling the entire space with a brilliant glow. It wasn't just a reflection of moonlight or will-o'-wisps anymore; it was as though the statues themselves had become vessels of divine light, the figure at the centre of the shrine shone brighter than the rest, almost as if it had come to life.

The three ladies, temporarily stunned by the brilliance, instinctively took a few steps back. From where they stood, just near the entrance of the inner shrine, they could take in the full view of the room. The statues—now glowing in their full glory—seemed to pulsate with energy. The once-still stone figures now had a vibrancy that made them seem as though they were part of something far beyond the physical world.

Then, the celestial beings—who had always seemed to stand guard at the edges of the shrine—moved forward. The hound, always the leader, entered first, walking with purposeful steps toward the statue at the centre. The bird, with its graceful wings, flew towards the Vishnu statue, while the feline moved toward the Buddha statue.

One by one, the animals disappeared inside the statues. It was as though they were absorbed into the stone itself, merging with the divine energy of the Gods they represented. The act was seamless and fluid, almost as though the animals themselves were divine extensions of the Gods, manifesting physically in their animal forms. The air seemed to hum with a new, almost sacred energy, and the three friends stood there in awe, unable to move or speak

For a long while, they stood in silence, the only sound being the faint echo of their own breathing as they processed the significance of what had just unfolded before them.

Just as they revelled in the magnificence of the event unfolding before them, a sudden and strong gust of wind swept into the shrine from the outside. It wasn't an ordinary breeze; it carried an intensity that seemed to shake the very ground that they were standing on. In an instant, their otherworldly vision—so vivid just moments ago—was taken from them. With their sight lost, everything went black.

CHAPTER 17

"I can't see anything," Smitha whispered, her voice trembling slightly.

"Neither can I," came Chandra's response, her tone was laced with confusion and unease.

"I cannot see anything!" Ayisha blurted out, her voice rising with panic.

Smitha could hear a rustling sound coming from Ayisha's direction. Alarmed, she realised what was happening. Without hesitation, she lunged to her left, where she knew Ayisha was standing. Her hands reached out blindly, colliding with Ayisha's shoulders. "Don't remove the blindfold!" she exclaimed, her voice cutting through the tense silence.

She could feel Ayisha fumbling with her blindfold, trying to pry it loose. "Don't!" Smitha whispered urgently into her friend's ear, her grip tightening around Ayisha, trying to give her a sense of comfort while holding her steady. Thankfully, Ayisha hadn't succeeded.

Smitha's thoughts darted to Chandra. "Chandra! Do you have your blindfold on?" she asked. She was panting, but her concern was evident.

"Yes, I do," Chandra replied, her voice tinged with uncertainty. "I don't want to risk being stunned or blinded..."

"But I don't know what to do," she admitted after a pause. "We're blind and in the middle of nowhere."

The three stood frozen, grappling with their fear. Their breaths were shallow, the oppressive darkness amplifying every sound and every movement. Smitha tightened her grip around Ayisha, anchoring herself and her friends in the midst of the chaos swirling within their minds

"Alright, here is the plan," Smitha said firmly, still holding Ayisha, whose uneven breathing betrayed her struggle to stay composed. "We'll turn towards the entrance, take a few steps to make sure we're facing the outside, then remove our blindfolds and step out. Let's not panic. I guess our job here is done, and that's why we've lost our powers."

Her words carried a calmness she didn't feel, but she knew she had to steady herself for the others.

Keeping Ayisha close, Smitha turned her around gently. She tightened her hold, wrapping her arm around Ayisha's shoulders, her touch both guiding and grounding. With her free hand, she reached out for Chandra, brushing against her trembling frame. Smitha rested her hand on Chandra's shoulder, squeezing it lightly in reassurance. "We've got this," she whispered.

The three of them moved in unison, their steps were slow and deliberate. The darkness pressed against them, making each moment feel heavier.

Suddenly, Ayisha stopped abruptly, her entire body tensing. "We're at the door," she whimpered, her voice barely audible. Her fear was evident, but Smitha could feel her fighting to hold it at bay.

"Good," Smitha whispered. "We're here," She steadied Ayisha, anchoring her against the fear threatening to overwhelm them all. Each step closer to safety was a victory, though the unknown still loomed ahead.

"Let us remove the blindfolds," said Smitha, her voice steady yet gentle, as though coaxing them back to reality.

Without hesitation, Ayisha yanked hers down, her breaths ragged and hurried. Smitha and Chandra followed more carefully, pulling off their blindfolds completely. As their eyes adjusted, the moonlight spilled across the scene, bathing the empty platforms in an ethereal glow. The faint shimmer of the platforms seemed almost alive, their long shadows shifting and quivering while whispering the remnants of their otherworldly encounter.

Grateful for the moonlight, Smitha took in the eerie quietness inside. *'At least we can see again,'* she thought, even if the vision brought an unsettling sense of desolation.

"Come on," Smitha urged softly, guiding the group to cross the doors of the inner shrine. They huddled close together as they walked out of the inner shrine. Their movements were cautious but determined.

The moment they stepped outside, a sharp gust of cold wind rushed past them as if trying to push them back in. Smitha's senses heightened as the rustling leaves and swaying trees came alive in a haunting rhythm, driven by a wind that was growing stronger by the second. The once tranquil forest now felt wild and untamed, as though it was responding to some unseen force.

"Stay close," Smitha said firmly, her voice barely rising above the wind but carrying enough strength to pull her friends' focus.

"Is it me, or is the wind blowing in circles... like *around* the shrine?" Chandra asked, her voice edged with unease. Without waiting for a response, she continued, "Let's move. We shouldn't stick around long enough to find out what this is."

Smitha nodded, though her attention was caught by the forest surrounding them. The path ahead was the only clear way forward; beyond it, the thick canopy of trees swallowed any light the moon offered. The dark silhouette of the forest loomed like a shadowy wall, impenetrable and oppressive. She shivered as goosebumps prickled her skin—a creeping sense of being watched was back, stronger than before.

She scanned her surroundings, her gaze darting from one patch of darkness to another. The forest seemed alive with an unnatural energy, but her city-dweller eyes, untrained in navigating such complete darkness, betrayed her. She could spot nothing out of the ordinary, but the feeling only deepened. '*Stay calm. Don't let fear show,*' she told herself.

Smitha's instincts screamed at her to stay silent, to not give away their presence. Tightening her hold on Ayisha, who was visibly trembling, and placing a reassuring hand on Chandra's shoulder, she guided them towards the opening in the wall. It was their only way out, their escape from whatever unseen force lingered.

Each step felt heavier than the last, the weight of the unknown pressing down on her. The rustling grew louder—behind them and ahead of them, like something—or someone—was moving on either end of the pathway. Her pulse quickened as her ears strained to make sense of the sounds, but the darkness refused to reveal its secrets.

"Torchli—" Ayisha began, but before she could finish, Smitha clamped her hand over her mouth, her movements quick and forceful. Smitha hadn't used the torchlight deliberately, knowing it could attract unwanted attention. She wanted them to remain unseen, blending into the shadows of the shrine.

But Ayisha's half-spoken word seemed to stir something. The rustling at the end of the pathway grew louder, sharper, as though *something* was now moving toward them. Smitha's heart raced, and she turned to Chandra, her panic reflected in Chandra's wide, terrified eyes.

Without speaking, Chandra grabbed Smitha's hand, and they darted toward the nearest platform—the one that had once cradled the mighty God's head. They crouched low, pressing themselves against the cold, ancient stone. The rough surface bit into their skin, but they hardly noticed. Their minds were consumed by the need to remain unseen. Their breathing was shallow, each inhale carefully controlled, as if any sound might betray their presence.

However, Ayisha couldn't shake the feeling that the platform was too small to shield all three of them. Her instincts screamed for space, for distance. Tugging herself free from Smitha's grip, she darted toward the adjacent platform. Her movements were quick but clumsy, her fear evident in the scuff of her shoes against the stone floor. Alone now, she crouched low, wrapping her arms tightly around her knees. Her breaths came in short, sharp bursts, each trembling gasp betraying her unease. Her hands clung to her sides as though shielding herself from the ominous unknown creeping ever closer.

The air around them shifted, growing thick and oppressive. The rustling that had once been distant now grew louder, sharper. It was no longer the wind teasing the leaves. It was deliberate. Purposeful. The sound of a predator closing in. Every sound—the rustling wind, the whisper of leaves, even their own muffled breaths— seemed magnified, reverberating through the stillness and filling the air with an unbearable tension.

Crouched behind the platform, Smitha strained her ears, trying to separate the noise from the pounding of her own heart. The forest, once alive with the endless symphony of crickets and croaking toads, had fallen into an unnatural silence. Even the wind, which had howled moments earlier, had stilled completely. The absence of sound was deafening, amplifying every small noise: the faint crunch of gravel underfoot, the brittle snap of a dry leaf breaking, and a dull, rhythmic thud that seemed to ebb and flow like a distant heartbeat.

Her throat tightened as a distinct sound mixed with the cacophony—a faint, almost imperceptible sound of loose gravel shifting with each step. It was subtle, yet it carried an unmistakable weight, as if something heavy was treading carefully yet inexorably toward her. *Thud, thud,* the rhythmic thud pressing against her ears like an ominous drumbeat.

The safety she felt behind the platform vanished when she heard the whispers of glass blades bending underfoot coming from all directions. They surrounded her, closing in from every side. The walls of the shrine seemed alive, their shadows stretching and shifting, swallowing what little light the moon offered. Smitha's breath hitched, and a cold sweat broke out across her skin. She felt exposed, vulnerable—a bait dangled before an unseen hunter.

Her mind raced with questions she didn't dare ask aloud. Who—or what—was circling them? And why did it feel as if the very shadows of the shrine sought to claim them?

Sensing danger from all directions, Smitha's instincts screamed for action. Against her better judgment, she decided to take a peek, her heart pounding like a war drum in her chest. Staying as low as possible, she craned her neck around the edge of the platform, her breath caught in her throat.

A tall figure emerged from the shadows near the shrine. His movements were deliberate, each step heavy with an eerie purpose. The moonlight cast faint glimmers on his form, and Smitha's stomach churned as recognition struck her. The figure wore old-fashioned garments that seemed to belong to another era, their folds flowing unnaturally with his steps. In his hand, he gripped a sword—an all-too-familiar blade.

Her eyes widened in disbelief, her thoughts racing. *Oh my god! It's the stone statue! The statue is walking!*

The divine reverence she had once felt for the shrine was utterly replaced by raw, primal fear. This was no longer a sacred protector; it was a predator, and she was its prey.

As if sensing her gaze, the creature paused. Its stone-like head turned slowly, unnervingly deliberate, until its hollow, lifeless eyes locked onto hers. Smitha froze. Her breath hitched as a cruel, menacing smile curled its lips. It was a smile devoid of humanity, a predator's grin that sent a shiver down her spine. The creature radiated malice, and Smitha felt her courage crumble under its weight.

The petrified figure's features were impossibly detailed, its stone body resembling flesh and sinew frozen in time. The realism was horrifying, as though the statue had never been stone at all but a living being petrified in a single, terrible moment.

The smile deepened as the figure raised its sword, the movement unnervingly smooth for something that should have been rigid. The blade gleamed faintly in the moonlight as it arced through the air in one swift, merciless swing.

Crash!

The sound was deafening, reverberating through the shrine like a thunderclap. The platform where Smitha had been crouching shattered into a shower of stone fragments. Dust and debris clouded the air as Smitha, acting purely on instinct, grabbed Chandra by the collar and yanked her backwards with all her strength. The force of her movement sent them both tumbling to the ground, their elbows taking the brunt of the fall.

They lay stunned, their breaths coming in sharp gasps, the reality of what had just happened sinking in. Smitha's hands trembled, her palms scraped and stinging. She didn't dare look up, afraid of what she might see. Beside her, Chandra was silent, her face pale and her eyes wide with terror.

On the adjacent platform, Ayisha had witnessed the entire scene unfold. Her hand clamped tightly over her mouth, muffling the scream that threatened to escape. Tears streamed down her cheeks, her body shaking as she fought to remain silent. The urge to cry out, to do *something*, was overwhelming, but fear rooted her in place. She clutched the edge of the platform as though it were her only anchor in a sea of chaos, her chest heaving with suppressed sobs.

Smitha's mind screamed for action, but her body felt paralysed. '*What now? What can we even do against that?*' She glanced toward Ayisha, whose terrified gaze met hers across the expanse of the shrine. Time felt frozen, but the danger was anything but that.

The creature stood amidst the debris of the shattered platform, its stone sword poised and its malevolent smile wider than before. It exuded an unnatural confidence as if savouring the hunt. The silence that followed the crash was heavier than the sound itself, broken only by the ragged breathing of the women and the faint rustle of disturbed leaves. The atmosphere seemed to thicken with malice, the air almost tangible with the intent to kill.

Smitha's heart pounded as she locked eyes with the creature. It wasn't just the horrifying reality of its form—it was the unmistakable *amusement* she saw in its stance. To it, they were nothing more than lively prey, and the thrill of the chase seemed to fuel its movements. The creature tilted its head slightly, its cold, lifeless eyes scanning the area, but before it could strike again, two new figures emerged from the darkness.

The Yakshas.

They moved with an eerie, robotic precision, their swords smaller and their motions slower than the creature's fluid and terrifying grace. The Yakshas, who had once stood guard over the shrine's gate, now seemed intent on confronting the malevolent figure. The man turned his gaze toward them, momentarily distracted. For a fleeting moment, Smitha dared to hope—but it didn't take long to realise the imbalance.

'*They're no match for him*', she thought, dread knotting her stomach. There was no emotion in the Yakshas' blank faces, no malice, no fear—just a lifeless determination. In stark contrast, the man radiated a savage will to kill. His aura was suffocating, primal, and overpowering.

As Smitha's eyes darted around the scene, her blood ran cold. Beyond the Yakshas and the man, she noticed a shadow moving along the edges of the shrine. It grew larger, and the sound of blades of grass rustling became louder, as though more figures were stirring in the darkness. The chilling realisation struck her. *The other statues—they're coming to life.*

'*I'm not staying to find out who's on whose side,*' she thought, her survival instincts taking over. Her eyes flicked towards the archway in the shrine wall. It was unguarded—a small but precious opportunity.

She glanced at Chandra, who was still crouched beside her. "This is our chance to run," Smitha whispered, her voice urgent but steady. She helped Chandra to her feet, gripping her arm tightly. "Go—head for the archway. Don't look back."

Without waiting for a response, Smitha darted toward Ayisha, who was still trembling behind the adjacent platform. Her heart ached for her friend, who seemed frozen in terror. Grabbing Ayisha's hand, she pulled hard, forcing her to her feet.

"Ayisha, *let's run!* Now is the chance!" Smitha shouted, her voice cutting through the oppressive silence. Her eyes darted back to Chandra, who had already started moving. "Go!" she yelled again, yanking Ayisha forward with every ounce of strength she could muster.

***

Chandra pelted towards the archway serving as the outer entrance. But before Chandra could reach the wall perimeter, her foot struck something hard and unyielding. She stumbled forward, her momentum sending her tumbling onto the rough ground. Pain shot through her leg like fire, forcing a gasp from her lips.

She looked down, clutching her throbbing leg, and froze. There, gripping her ankle with surprising strength, was a tiny stone man. He had six arms, a round belly, a thick moustache that curled upward, and a wild, toothy grin etched into his rocky face. Chandra's breath hitched. The carvings—the intricate, ancient figures adorning the inner shrine's walls—had come to life.

The rustling in the underbrush was no longer abstract or distant. It was the sound of countless tiny stone figures scuttling toward her, their jagged limbs scraping against the ground. Fear wrapped itself around her chest like a vice. She tried to pry the little man off, digging her nails into its rough surface, but its grip was unrelenting.

Desperate, Chandra swung her backpack at it with all her strength. The impact sent a dull *thud* reverberating through her arms, but the stone figure remained unmoved, its mocking grin unwavering. Panic clawed at her throat as the rustling grew closer, the sounds multiplying as if an army of these creatures was closing in.

In a final act of desperation, she lifted her trapped leg and slammed it against the rocky ground as hard as she could. The impact was jarring, sending shocks up her body, but it worked. The stone man's arms cracked and shattered, freeing her leg.

Just as she scrambled to her feet, she spotted Smitha rushing toward her, her face pale with panic, tears streaming down her cheeks. "Chandra!" Smitha's voice cracked with fear as she reached out, grabbing her by the arm and pulling her upright.

Chandra winced as pain shot through her leg again, but she forced herself to stand. Her eyes darted toward the shrine, taking in the chaos she had left behind. The Yakshas were still engaged with the larger creature, but one had fallen. Its body lay in a heap near the shattered remnants of the platform. The second Yakshan fought valiantly, but it was clear it was no match for the man with the stone sword.

Her gaze swept over the scattered debris—the piles of rubble from the platforms—and the creeping figures emerging from the shadows. It hit her with stark clarity: *We're the only ones left running.*

"Ayisha?" Chandra cried.

Smitha shook her head. Her eyes, filled with a deep sadness, answered all of Chandra's questions. Chandra's world crashed with a single expression from Smitha.

Smitha's grip tightened on Chandra's arm. "Come on! We have to move!"

With adrenaline fuelling their battered bodies, they pushed forward, sprinting toward the exit. The moment their feet crossed the threshold of the shrine's ancient walls, the rustling behind them seemed to intensify as though the creatures were enraged by their escape.

***

Smitha's heart sank when she saw Ayisha, crouched behind the platform, her face streaked with tears, her body trembling. Chandra had already reacted, darting away as soon as she realised the peril they were in. But Ayisha was frozen, unable to move, her terror locking her in place.

A wave of urgency swept over Smitha. She dashed towards Ayisha, grabbing her hands and yanking her upwards. "Ayisha, *let's run!* Now is the chance!" she shouted, her voice sharp with panic.

Ayisha didn't respond. Her eyes were wide, unblinking, and full of terror. They weren't hidden anymore. Smitha's stomach churned as she saw the tall man, still locked in battle with the two Yakshas, turn his gaze toward them.

'*No! We need to act fast!*' Smitha thought, her heart hammering in her chest.

Without thinking, she slapped Ayisha hard, the sound of it echoing in the tense silence. Ayisha blinked rapidly, her frozen expression faltering. Smitha saw her friend's gaze slowly clear. "Come! We don't have time—we need to get out of here!" she screamed.

The slap had done its work. Ayisha nodded, slowly rising to her feet, though her legs wobbled as if they hadn't the strength to carry her. Smitha grabbed her hand again, urgency in her movements.

Smitha pulled Ayisha toward the entryway, their only path to safety, but Ayisha's legs gave way once again. In the panic of the moment, Smitha's sweaty grip slipped. The force of the pull sent her tumbling to the ground.

And then it happened.

Crash!

Smitha's eyes widened in horror as she saw Ayisha engulfed by a cascade of rocks. The man had thrown one of the Yakshas onto the platform with such force that it shattered, sending debris flying. Smitha had barely dodged the attack by a heartbeat.

For a moment, everything seemed to freeze as Smitha stared, helpless, at the mound of rocks covering her friend. The earth beneath Ayisha's body darkened, drenched in the sickening red of blood. Smitha's stomach churned, the weight of the situation crashing into her. "No..." she wailed, her voice breaking with disbelief.

Her hands trembled as she frantically dug through the rocks, trying to free her friend, but the stone was too heavy, and her vision blurred from tears.

Then something strange happened. A faint glow emanated from within the rocks, a soft light pulsing through the damp earth. Slowly, more glowing balls of light began to rise from the dark soil, moving toward the tall man. The lights swirled around him, entering his body, feeding into him as if he were absorbing their essence.

We are the sacrifices. The thought hit Smitha with chilling clarity. That's why he was after them—their deaths had been the purpose all along. Ayisha was gone.

Grief and terror gripped her chest, but there was no time to mourn. Smitha pushed herself up, a sharp breath catching in her throat. She turned and bolted toward the exit, her mind racing with the need to escape.

Ahead of her, she saw Chandra on the ground, struggling against something, her body caught in the chaos. Without hesitation, Smitha rushed to help her, pulling her to her feet. Together, they stumbled towards the exit, their only remaining chance for survival.

Chapter 18

Once beyond the shrine's walls, Chandra and Smitha collapsed behind the crumbled barrier, gasping for air. Their bodies trembled from the adrenaline coursing through them, their chests heaving as they tried to calm their pounding hearts. They wanted to keep running but found themselves immobilised—exhaustion anchoring them in place.

Peering cautiously through the cracks in the wall, they could see the tiny stone statues filling the shrine. The grotesque figures scuttled and crept, their eerie movements mechanical yet lifelike. However, none of them ventured beyond the shrine's boundary as though an invisible barrier held them within. The sight brought a fleeting sense of relief.

After what felt like an eternity but could only have been a few moments, Chandra straightened. "We need to move," she whispered hoarsely, the urgency in her voice cutting through their momentary reprieve. Smitha nodded, her limbs heavy and her mind dulled by the loss of her friend.

They started towards the pathway they had come in through, the one familiar route that seemed like their only lifeline.

"Boom! Rumble... Crash!"

The deafening sound froze them in their tracks.

Before their eyes, the wall ahead of them erupted in a cascade of debris. Dust and stone filled the air as the remnants of the final Yakshan's defeat became clear. The creature had been hurled against the wall with such force that it disintegrated on impact, the shockwave obliterating both the Yakshan and the structure itself.

A mountain of jagged rocks now blocked the path, spilling across the ground and sealing off their escape route.

"No," Smitha whispered, dread clawing at her chest. Her eyes, filled with tears, darted to the dense forest surrounding them. The thorny undergrowth and towering evergreens loomed like an unyielding fortress. The forest was untouched, wild, and utterly impenetrable. There was no way to go around the blocked path.

Chandra's gaze followed Smitha's, her face pale and drawn. "What do we do now?" she breathed, her voice trembling.

Through the gaping hole in the wall, Smitha's worst fear came to life. She could see it clearly—the tall, malicious figure stepping forward, its movements unnaturally smooth yet deliberate.

The creature's eyes glinted in the moonlight. Its smile was even crueller than before. It carried the weight of triumph, knowing its prey was now cornered.

Smitha grabbed Chandra's arm, her nails digging into her friend's skin. "We can't let him catch us," she whispered fiercely, her voice quaking with equal parts fear and determination. *'I am not going to lose another friend.'*

Desperate, Smitha scanned the area for any other escape routes. Her eyes landed on a faint trail diverging from the shrine, weaving upwards into the dense forest. "Let's go this way," she said hurriedly, pointing toward the path. "It seems to lead to the hilltop. From there, we can figure out a way back toward the park."

Chandra, still panting heavily, managed only a nod. Words felt like a luxury she couldn't afford as exhaustion weighed heavily on her.

Without further delay, they bolted toward the narrow footpath. Unlike the pathway they had initially taken, this one was overgrown and treacherous, as though nature itself was trying to reclaim it. The uneven trail forced them to slow down, their escape becoming more of a struggle with each step.

The deeper they went, the denser the forest became. The towering trees of the evergreen jungle interlocked their canopies, plunging the trail into near darkness. Thorny bushes lined the path, scraping their exposed skin and leaving thin trails of blood on their hands and arms. Each scratch stung, but neither of them dared to stop.

Smitha led the way, using her arms to push aside the encroaching branches and thorns, creating a makeshift path for them to pass through. Sweat trickled down her face as she fought against the unrelenting wilderness, her breaths quick and shallow.

Chandra trailed close behind, her legs throbbing with pain. Every step sent jolts of agony up her body, but her determination to survive burned brighter than her discomfort. She wanted to help Smitha clear the path, knowing it would speed up their desperate journey. Yet she couldn't bring herself to take the lead—her body was too battered, her strength waning.

'If I fall or falter, Smitha will have to carry me,' Chandra thought grimly. She clenched her fists, pushing herself forward with sheer willpower.

The forest seemed to close in around them, the oppressive darkness swallowing the faint moonlight entirely. The only sounds were the crunch of their footsteps on the undergrowth and the occasional rustle of unseen creatures in the distance.

"Careful!" Smitha whispered harshly as her foot slipped on a loose patch of earth. She caught herself on a nearby tree trunk, its bark rough against her palms. Turning to check on Chandra, she saw the strain etched on her friend's face but said nothing. Words of concern or encouragement would feel hollow in their current situation.

Every scrape, every stumble, and every strained breath served as a cruel reminder of how far they were from safety.

***

At a distance, the creature loomed near the ruins of the shrine, its expression unreadable yet charged with malice. It scanned the surroundings, its stone-carved face twisting slightly as though sniffing out the women who had fled.

Its gaze shifted toward the path leading away from the shrine. The moonlight bathed the forest in silvery light, and for a moment, everything seemed still. Then, as if answering an unspoken wish, the trail the women had taken began to shimmer faintly—a pulsating glow that moved rhythmically, like a beacon guiding the way.

The creature tilted its head skyward, its humanoid features illuminated by the moonlight. There was an unnatural reverence in the gesture as if it were invoking an unseen power. Slowly, it lowered its gaze back to the glowing path. Recognition flickered in its cold, stony eyes. The faint glow faded just as abruptly as it had appeared, but it was enough.

With deliberate precision, the creature began moving toward the path. Each step was heavy, leaving deep indents in the ground as though the earth itself recoiled from its weight. The sound of its movements—a mix of grinding stone and the dull thud of impact—echoed faintly in the stillness of the forest.

Trailing behind it was a swarm of tiny stone creatures, their jagged forms scuttling around the shrine's perimeter like restless insects. They clawed and scratched at the invisible barrier that confined them, their frustration manifesting in sharp, grating noises. No matter how they tried, they couldn't breach the boundary, their movements frantic yet futile.

Unbothered by their limitations, the larger creature pressed forward, its slow, unyielding pace exuding an air of inevitability. It seemed to know that its prey couldn't run forever.

CHAPTER 19

Smitha and Chandra had been trudging along the narrow trail for what felt like hours, their legs screaming for rest, their lungs burning with each ragged breath. Yet, they knew better than to stop. Stopping meant certain death.

The forest seemed to grow denser with each step. The thorny underbrush tore at their clothes and skin, leaving angry red marks, but neither dared to complain. Their focus was on survival, on the faint hope that the trail might lead to safety.

Suddenly, the stillness shattered.

Crash.

Chandra froze, her blood running cold. "It's following us," she whispered, her voice trembling with fear. She didn't need to look back to know the truth. The crashing sounds were unmistakable. The creature, too large for the narrow trail, was cutting its own path through the forest, its strength evident in the destruction it left behind.

Smitha clenched her fists, forcing her panic down. "Then let's leave the path," she said, her voice firm despite the terror gnawing at her. "We'll head west, straight through the forest. It'll be harder for it to follow us that way."

Without waiting for a reply, Smitha fumbled with her phone, her fingers trembling as she pulled up the compass app. The screen's faint glow illuminated their faces, pale with exhaustion and fear.

"West is this way," Smitha said, pointing.

Chandra nodded weakly, leaning on Smitha for support as they veered off the trail and plunged into the forest's untamed depths. The foliage grew thicker, the trees taller, their ancient roots snaking across the uneven ground. Each step was a battle against the terrain, but they pushed forward, driven by the sound of the relentless destruction behind them.

Minutes stretched into what felt like hours. Every rustle, every shadow seemed like a harbinger of doom. The forest felt alive, conspiring against them.

Finally, they emerged into a small clearing, only to be met with yet another obstacle.

A tall metal fence loomed before them, its wires twisted into a sturdy mesh that stretched high into the night. Smitha stopped abruptly, her chest heaving as she stared at the barrier in disbelief.

"No..." Chandra's voice broke as she staggered to the ground, her knees giving way under the weight of despair. "No, no, no!" she wailed, clutching at the dirt.

There was no gate in sight, no gap to squeeze through. The fence stood like an unyielding sentinel, its purpose clear: to keep people—and creatures—out. Or, in their case, to keep them trapped.

They were cornered, like moths in a jar, their fluttering wings brushing ever closer to the flame.

Crash.

Another tree fell, closer this time. The sound jolted them both, pulling them out of their momentary despair.

Chandra's tear-filled eyes darted to Smitha, whose expression had turned grim. The ground seemed to vibrate slightly beneath their feet, a foreboding reminder of the creature's immense weight.

"It's coming," Smitha said, her voice barely above a whisper. The words hung in the air, heavy and final.

They had no time to think, no time to plan. They could hear it now—the dull thud of the creature's footsteps, the snapping of branches as it moved, bound to them by some unseen force.

They were out of time.

"Let's walk along the fence," Smitha suggested, her voice was steady though her heart pounded like a drum. "Maybe we'll reach the hilltop. The fence there seemed low enough to jump over."

Her survival instincts had finally surged, drowning out the suffocating waves of despair. She felt a fierce determination to see Chandra to safety—even if she couldn't save herself.

Chandra nodded weakly, clutching Smitha's hand as they started moving. Smitha led the way, her eyes scanning the path ahead while her free hand brushed aside low-hanging branches and vines.

The ground near the fence was clearer, with less vegetation, allowing them to move faster. But this came at a cost. They both knew the creature would face less resistance here, too. Each crack of a branch or distant crash of a tree was a stark reminder of their pursuer's relentless approach.

"We can't stop," Smitha muttered, more to herself than to Chandra. Her grip tightened around her friend's hand as if tethering Chandra to her resolve.

After what felt like an eternity, they reached a rocky clearing. The dense forest gave way to uneven stones that shimmered faintly under the moonlight.

Smitha and Chandra exchanged a glance, their breaths coming in ragged gasps.

"This is it," Smitha whispered, the first spark of hope glinting in her eyes

The rocky outcrop led to a small section of fence perched atop the rocks, and beyond that stood the hilltop. She could make out the silhouette of the canteen. Hopefully, there is an emergency staircase—a pathway to safety and, perhaps, the city beyond.

"We can do this," Smitha said, more firmly this time.

Guiding Chandra with care, Smitha stepped onto the first rock. She tested its stability before motioning for Chandra to follow. Slowly, painstakingly, they climbed. Smitha would pause to help Chandra over larger stones, her hands steady even as her legs threatened to buckle under exhaustion.

Finally, they reached the top. The fence here was mercifully low. With one final effort, they clambered over it and landed on the other side, collapsing onto the grassy hilltop.

For a moment, neither of them moved. Their chests heaved as they gasped for air, sweat mixing with the dirt and blood that clung to their scraped skin. The cool night breeze kissed their faces, a small reprieve from the suffocating humidity of the forest.

Smitha was the first to sit up. She turned towards the vast hillside they had just crossed, her eyes scanning the dark expanse.

Smitha realised they had finally gained the upper hand. From the hilltop, the full moon's silvery glow illuminated the landscape, revealing details that had been hidden in the dense forest below. Her eyes followed the steep rocky slope they had just climbed. The incline was sharp and unforgiving, its surface smooth and treacherous. A smile of triumph crept onto her face.

There's no way that petrified creature can climb this. Not with its stony hands and rocky legs.

She glanced at Chandra, who was catching her breath beside her. Chandra's face mirrored her relief, a flicker of hope breaking through their shared exhaustion.

Smitha's gaze swept across the hillside, following the path of destruction the creature had left in its wake. Uprooted trees and jagged shadows marked its trail. She thought she could finally breathe.

But the relief was short-lived.

"Look," Smitha whispered, her voice tight with dread as she pointed towards a shadowed section of the hillside.

Chandra followed Smitha's line of sight, her eyes widening as they settled on what appeared to be a fallen fence. The wire-mesh barrier that marked the park's boundary lay crumpled, twisted unnaturally. Beyond it, the dark silhouette of the creature stood still, ominous and out of place within the carefully maintained grounds of the park. The park's well-trodden paths and open grounds now offered it a clear advantage.

"It's ahead of us," Smitha murmured, the pit of her stomach sinking.

Chandra's breath hitched. "How—how did it get there so fast?"

"I don't know," Smitha replied, her mind racing. She felt the weight of the realisation pressing down on her. They were no longer running from the creature; it had circled them in. And worse, it was now inside the very place they'd hoped would offer safety.

Smitha clenched her fists, forcing herself to think. "We need to move now," she said, her voice steady despite the panic threatening to overwhelm her. Without waiting for a response, she grabbed Chandra's arm and pulled her towards the nearest building.

"Stay close," Chandra whispered, her voice barely audible.

Smitha glanced back at Chandra, her expression resolute. '*We'll figure out an escape, but we can't stop now.*'

The two friends huddled on the terrace of the building, which also served as the hilltop, their breaths shallow and hearts pounding. From their vantage point, the park sprawled below, moonlight casting eerie shadows across the grounds.

"What do we do now?" Chandra whispered, her voice low yet trembling with panic. She glanced towards the park grounds, where the dark creature prowled ominously. "We can't run across. That *thing* is already there."

Smitha clenched her fists, her hope flickering. "Do you think we can outrun it?" she asked, desperation creeping into her tone.

Chandra shook her head firmly, her gaze darting around for an alternative. "No. It's too tall, too strong. We'll be overpowered in seconds." Her mind raced, unwilling to let fear paralyse her. *There has to be a way out of this.*

Smitha edged cautiously towards the fence, her movements deliberate to avoid making noise. Peering out, she scanned the park below. Her stomach twisted as she spotted the creature—a looming shadow against the faint silver glow of the moon.

"It's still coming," Smitha muttered, more to herself than to Chandra. The creature's relentless pursuit was unnerving, its movement precise, as if tethered to them by some unseen force. Each step it took seemed calculated, closing the distance with an inevitability that made her blood run cold.

"We can't stay here," Chandra said, her voice barely audible but laced with determination. Her eyes darted to the surrounding terrain, calculating risks, searching for possibilities. "We need to think fast."

Smitha looked at Chandra, her face resolute despite the fear flickering in her eyes. "I've got an idea," she said, crouching beside her. "This thing—it's ancient, right? A thousand years old, at least. I'm betting brute force is its main strength. It doesn't look like it can fly, but I'm sure it can see and hear way better than we can in the dark."

Chandra raised an eyebrow, her voice strained with frustration. "So? Why are you stating the obvious?"

Smitha leaned in, her voice dropping further. "Because that's exactly how we can outwit it. Have you noticed how it always walks straight towards us, like some kind of compass locked in our direction?"

Chandra frowned, realisation beginning to dawn. "You think it's tracking us somehow?"

"Exactly," Smitha continued, her voice growing more determined. "We need to use that against it. Let's switch on everything we can in this building—all the noisy machines and contraptions. The sound and chaos should disorient it. Once it climbs up to investigate, we'll bolt down the emergency stairs."

Chandra hesitated, glancing towards the shadowy figure below. "And what if it takes the stairs too? It might be smarter than it looks."

Smitha nodded, acknowledging the risk. "True. But it'll take time for it to decide or even break through the building to get out. That time could give us the edge we need to put more distance between us and it."

Chandra exhaled sharply, nodding as her lips tightened into a grim line. "Okay, it's not perfect, but it's something. Let's do it."

"Alright," Smitha said, her voice steady despite the chaos in her mind. "I saw that each floor has a main switch. I'll go down and start with the ground floor, then work my way up, switching everything on as I go." She paused, glancing at Chandra. "You stay here. Save your energy for the final sprint."

Chandra shook her head, her expression firm. "No. I'll check the emergency staircase to make sure it's not locked or blocked. Better safe than sorry."

Smitha's eyes widened in alarm, and she grabbed Chandra's arm instinctively. "No!" she exclaimed, her voice cracking with desperation. "That staircase is *outside* the building! It's too dangerous." Her hands trembled as she clung to Chandra's arm. "I—I can't lose you too," she whispered, her voice barely audible, trembling under the weight of their shared loss.

Chandra's face softened, and for a moment, the harsh determination in her eyes gave way to warmth. She gently placed her hand over Smitha's. "We'll both get out of this alive," she said softly. Then, pulling her arm free, she added, "This is the best way to make sure of that."

Smitha opened her mouth to protest again, but Chandra was already stepping away towards the emergency staircase. Her movements were deliberate, her resolve unshakable. She turned back once, a small smile tugging at her lips. "Trust me," she said, her voice filled with quiet confidence.

Smitha froze, watching her friend disappear into the shadows. Her hand lingered in the air as though trying to grasp something already out of reach. Her knees buckled slightly, and tears welled up, blurring her vision. "Chandra..." she whispered, her voice breaking.

But Chandra was gone.

Swallowing the lump in her throat, Smitha clenched her fists and turned back towards the terrace door. The cool metal of the door handle steadied her resolve as she gripped it tightly. *'The faster I switch everything on, the safer she'll be,'* she thought, forcing herself to focus.

Wiping away her tears with the back of her hand, Smitha pushed against the terrace door. It didn't budge. Her breath hitched as she realised—it was locked, an old-fashioned bolt barring her way. Panic threatened to bubble up, but she forced herself to think. Spotting a rock and a sturdy stick nearby, she jammed them into the crevice and used all her strength to pry the door open. The rusty bolt gave way with a jarring screech that echoed in the night, setting her heart racing.

With the path cleared, she stepped inside the darkened building, the air heavy and still. Her torchlight cut through the gloom, illuminating the narrow stairwell ahead. Determination burned in her chest, its heat pushing back the fear that threatened to overwhelm her. Gripping the torch tightly, she began her descent, her footsteps echoing softly in the confined space as she moved towards the switches—and survival.

CHAPTER 20

Chandra moved down the emergency staircase with deliberate care, each step measured to avoid making any noise. The metal staircase spiralled down the side of the building, with openings leading onto balconies on every floor. She paused at each landing, quietly inspecting the balconies. The large windows provided potential entry points, allowing them to jump from the balcony onto the emergency stairs if needed.

Her descent continued, her injured leg throbbing with every step. She grits her teeth, determined not to let the pain slow her down. When she finally reached the ground floor, she took a moment to assess her surroundings. The emergency staircase opened directly onto the park grounds, unobstructed by debris or barriers. From here, she traced the route they'd need to take—straight across the open expanse of the park to the massive red gates. But they would have to climb over the gates to escape.

Her eyes drifted to her leg. The sharp, relentless ache was a stark reminder of her limits. She knew she was pushing her body far beyond its capacity, but this wasn't the time to falter. A grim thought crossed her mind— she might not outrun the creature. But if she could buy Smitha enough time to escape, it would be worth it.

Satisfied with her reconnaissance, Chandra turned and began her ascent. She pushed herself to move quickly despite her injury, her ears straining for any sign of movement. The plan relied on timing, and she knew the countdown would begin the moment Smitha activated the first main switch. It wouldn't be long now.

As she neared the second floor, the entire park suddenly lit up, bathing the grounds in stark, artificial light. A cacophony of loud music erupted, echoing through the night. Chandra froze for a heartbeat, the sudden brightness and noise catching her off guard.

'*Smitha's started switching everything on,*' she thought, her pulse quickening. The creature would notice immediately.

Pushing past the burning pain in her leg, she quickened her pace, climbing the stairs two at a time despite the protest of her exhausted body. She needed to make it back to the terrace—the starting point of their desperate gambit.

***

It took Smitha some time to figure out the building's controls, but her determination didn't waver. Each switch panel was old and slightly rusted, the labels barely legible. She carefully memorised the controls during her descent to the ground floor. The first switch was located near the main entrance, and after flipping it on, the ground floor lit up, flooding the area with light.

Without wasting a second, Smitha sprinted up the stairs, quickly activating the switches on each floor. The faint hum of electricity rose with every level, accompanied by the whirring of old machinery and the occasional flicker of light. By the time the building was fully illuminated, she was panting heavily but resolutely.

She pushed open the terrace door, her heart lifting with relief when she saw Chandra waiting for her.

Chandra immediately pointed to a small service ladder leading to the roof. "Let's climb this. From up there, we'll have a clear view of the building's entrance and the surrounding area," she said, her voice low but firm.

Smitha nodded, following Chandra up the ladder. The climb was short but felt longer due to the weight of the moment. Once on the rooftop, the two women crouched low, scanning the park grounds. With the lights illuminating the area, they quickly spotted the massive stone creature.

The statue-like being lumbered near the building, its hulking frame casting long, distorted shadows across the park. It moved slowly along the walls, smashing them in places as if testing for weak spots. Each strike echoed ominously, a reminder of the destruction it was capable of.

"It's checking the walls," Smitha whispered, her eyes wide with alarm.

Chandra nodded grimly. "It's near the lobby," she said, pointing towards the creature's path. Past the lobby lay the wooden doors guarding the main entrance.

The women watched as the creature disappeared from their line of sight, moving further along the building. Chandra held her breath, waiting a few moments before signalling to Smitha.

"Now," she mouthed, motioning towards the service ladder.

The two descended swiftly and silently, their movements feeling almost rehearsed in their urgency. Chandra led the way to the second-floor balcony, her steps careful yet brisk. Smitha followed closely, gripping the railing for support. The cool night air pressed against them, and every creak of the emergency stairs felt amplified.

They paused on the balcony, straining their ears for any sign of the creature amidst the chaos. The blaring park music and flickering lights created an unsettling atmosphere, making it difficult to discern distant sounds.

Then— *CRASH!*

A deafening noise shattered through the chaos, echoing up from below. Smitha and Chandra froze, their eyes wide as they exchanged a look of both fear and grim relief. Their trap had worked.

"It's in," Chandra whispered, her voice barely audible over the pounding in her chest.

They crouched low, peering cautiously over the balcony railing. Below, faint shadows danced erratically, accompanied by the metallic groans of the building straining under the creature's weight.

"All we need to do now is wait," Smitha murmured, her voice steady despite the tension tightening her throat. "The moment it climbs to the second floor, we'll run down the emergency stairs."

Chandra glanced at the narrow staircase, its flimsy metal frame trembling faintly in the breeze. For the first time, she felt a pang of gratitude for its poor construction.

"It won't hold if it tries to follow us," she muttered, half to herself.

Her words hung in the air, a sliver of hope laced with dread. If the creature caught on to their plan or moved faster than anticipated, their window of escape would vanish.

Smitha's ears caught the sound of shattering glass, followed by an electronic voice cheerfully declaring a winner amidst triumphant music. Her stomach churned as realisation dawned. "The creature has entered the building," she whispered, her voice barely audible. The funhouse's automated system had been triggered.

A second crash reverberated through the air, followed by an eerie silence. Even the music seemed to waver and fade slightly, the cheerful tone morphing into something ominous against the backdrop of destruction.

She strained to listen. Random piano notes began to play, their haunting discord breaking the quiet, while motion-activated voices of animated characters cackled and squeaked in fragmented phrases. The chaotic symphony was punctuated by more crashes, the sound of furniture or displays being thrown about with reckless force.

"Get ready," Smitha hissed, her voice tight with dread. She was sure the creature was just one floor below.

The two ducked behind the wall, pressing their backs into the cold concrete. They could hear their own ragged breathing echo in the confined space, but neither dared to move. Smitha reached out and gently tugged Chandra further into the shadows, her fingers trembling but firm.

Her mind raced, a silent vow forming: *It won't find us easily. Whatever edge we have, we'll use it.*

The pounding of heavy footsteps began to resonate through the building, each one louder than the last. The sound wasn't hurried but deliberate, the slow and steady gait of a predator that knew its prey had nowhere to run.

Smitha's gaze locked on the wall in front of her, watching as shadows flickered and danced, distorted by the erratic park lighting. Suddenly, a faint blue glow appeared, its light reflecting on the wall. The familiar jingle of the funhouse echoed, warped and hollow in the oppressive silence.

"Now," Smitha whispered urgently.

Without hesitation, she and Chandra bolted down the emergency staircase. Their footsteps clanged noisily on the metal stairs, no longer concerned with stealth. The creature was too close, and the game had shifted. This wasn't hide-and-seek anymore—it was a desperate game of tag.

Each step felt heavier as adrenaline surged through their veins, urging them forward. The sound of their frantic descent echoed around them, blending with the distorted cacophony of the funhouse. The cold air stung their faces, and their lungs burned with exertion, but they didn't dare slow down.

Above them, the crashing and chaos continued, each sound a grim reminder of how close the danger was. Smitha spared a glance at Chandra, her friend's face set with determination despite the fear in her eyes. Neither of them said a word, their unspoken resolve keeping them moving.

Smitha grabbed Chandra's hand as they reached the bottom of the stairs, pulling her forward without breaking stride. The two of them sprinted towards the red gate that enclosed the park, their footsteps pounding against the ground. Behind them, pieces of the stone wall shattered with deafening force, the destruction echoing ominously in the night.

They were halfway to the gate when a loud metallic *clang* pierced the air. Instinctively, Smitha glanced back. Her heart skipped a beat as she saw the metal emergency stairs lying crumpled on the ground, twisted and broken. Above it, a dark silhouette loomed in the balcony, motionless but menacing, its gaze fixed squarely on them.

The building behind the creature was in ruins. Broken glass panes glinted in the dim light, the entrance door lay shattered, and jagged holes gaped in the stone walls. For a brief moment, relief washed over Smitha—the plan had worked. The creature was delayed, even if just for a moment.

"Come on!" she urged, gripping Chandra's arm tighter as they pushed forward. Their breaths came in ragged gasps as they approached the towering red gate.

"Climb up first. I'll give you a boost and follow you," Smitha said hurriedly, her eyes darting over her shoulder to check the creature's position. The balcony was empty. Her stomach clenched—it was already on the move.

"No, you go first!" Chandra insisted, her voice sharp with urgency.

"Just go! No time to argue!" Smitha snapped, giving Chandra a firm shove towards the gate.

Reluctantly, Chandra obeyed, gripping the cold iron bars and beginning her climb. The gate was tall and slippery with dew, but adrenaline powered her movements. Smitha crouched beneath her, bracing herself to boost her friend up further.

Once Chandra reached the top, she swung her legs over and began to climb down the other side. Her injured leg throbbed painfully with each movement, but she gritted her teeth and jumped to the ground. As she landed, a flicker of movement caught her eye.

"It's at the door!" she yelled, panic thick in her voice.

Smitha didn't look back. "Take out the scooter keys while I come down!" she shouted, already scrambling up the gate. Her fingers dug into the bars as she climbed, her arms straining with the effort.

Chandra's trembling hands fumbled in her pocket, eventually finding the keys. Without wasting a second, she sprinted towards the parked scooters. Her breath came in short, desperate bursts, the looming shadow of the creature spurring her forward.

Behind her, Smitha reached the top of the gate. She stole a glance at the building. The dark figure now stood at the threshold of the ruined doorway, its glowing eyes locked onto her. For a moment, time seemed to slow. Then, with renewed urgency, Smitha swung her legs over the gate and began her descent.

Smitha had climbed down by then, pausing for just a moment to glance back at the creature. It was moving steadily, its massive legs covering the ground alarmingly fast despite the deliberate pace. It wasn't running—yet—but that offered little comfort. They couldn't hope to outrun it on foot. Their only chance was the scooter.

The park lights illuminated the creature's face as it emerged fully into view. The earlier glint of predatory joy had vanished, replaced by something far more terrifying—the fury of a devil unleashed. Its rage burned through the dark hollows of its eyes, a fury so raw that Smitha felt her stomach churn. She didn't linger. With her heart pounding in her chest, she turned and sprinted towards the scooter.

Chandra was already astride the scooter, the engine sputtering to life as she balanced on one foot, ready to move. The moment Smitha slid into the seat behind her, Chandra twisted the throttle. The scooter jerked forward, accelerating away from the building.

"Keep looking behind you!" Chandra yelled over the engine's hum, her voice firm despite the strain in her tone.

"Yes," Smitha replied breathlessly, gripping Chandra tightly as she glanced back. Her eyes widened in alarm. Behind them, the metal gate groaned, then clanged violently. The creature was through.

Chandra pushed the scooter to its limit, the wind whipping against their faces as they raced away. The looming outline of the park and its towering gates faded into the distance. For the first time in what felt like an eternity, they saw the lights of the city ahead.

Relief washed over them as they crossed into the city grounds. The hum of life—distant traffic, faint streetlights—wrapped around them like a comforting embrace. They didn't dare stop, but the oppressive weight of fear began to lift.

For now, they were alive. For now, they had escaped.

***

By dawn, they were seated in the bustling airport terminal, the bright lights and constant announcements a stark contrast to the horrors they had narrowly escaped. The chaos of travellers rushing about felt surreal, almost as if the world had moved on while they were trapped in a nightmare.

As they waited with their last-minute tickets, Smitha broke the silence, her voice barely above a whisper. "I wish we could've done something for her."

Chandra didn't need to ask who. Ayisha's absence loomed between them, a weight neither could shake off. She simply nodded while her tired eyes fixed on the flickering departure board.

Words felt unnecessary after that. The exhaustion etched on their faces spoke louder than any conversation. When their flight was called, they rose in silence, each step feeling heavier yet laced with the faintest hint of hope.

As the plane ascended, Smitha found herself staring out of the window. The island grew smaller and smaller, its ominous shadows dissolving into the vast expanse of the horizon. The nightmare, tethered to that cursed place, seemed to shrink with it.

Smitha reached for Chandra's hand, squeezing it gently as the tension finally began to ease. "We made it," she whispered, more to herself than anyone else.

Chandra gave a faint smile, the first in what felt like forever. They were finally free.